# FRAN

## 1930

*A new version of*
*Mary Wollstonecraft Shelley's book*

*adapted for the stage by*

## Fred Carmichael

# SAMUEL FRENCH, INC.
**45 WEST 25TH STREET**  **NEW YORK 10010**
**7623 SUNSET BOULEVARD**  **HOLLYWOOD 90046**
*LONDON*  *TORONTO*

ISBN 0 573 69588 1          Printed in U.S.A.          # 8196

## IMPORTANT BILLING AND CREDIT REQUIREMENTS

All producers of FRANKENSTEIN 1930 *must* give credit to the Author of the Play in all programs distributed in connection with performances of the Play and in all instances in which the title of the Play appears for purposes of advertising, publicizing or otherwise exploiting the Play and/or a production. The name of the Author *must* also appear on a separate line, on which no other name appears, immediately following the title, and *must* appear in size of type not less than fifty percent the size of the title type.

FRANKENSTEIN 1930 was first produced at the Fort Salem Theatre in Salem, N.Y. on July 12, 1995.

## FRANKENSTEIN 1930

*Adapted from Mary Wollstonecraft Shelley's book
by Fred Carmichael*

Directed by Quentin C. Beaver

| | |
|---|---|
| Mother | Krishna Judkins |
| Daughter | Mary Francis |
| Grave Diggers | Gabriel Byer |
| | & Jeremy Bellrose |
| Victor Frankenstein | Bill Mutimer |
| Gorgo | Jason Taylor |
| Aunt Frederica | Nancy Simmons |
| Berta | Liza Nicolai |
| Henry Lovitz | Tim Johnson |
| Dr. Hellstrom | Thomas Nichols |
| The Creature | Fred Carmichael |
| Horst | Gabriel Byer |
| Jalna | Kirshna Judkins |
| Second Man | Jeremy Bellrose |
| Maria | Meredith Schultens |
| | *(alternate Elizabeth Green)* |
| Korda | K.T. Miner |

The action of the play takes place outside of Vienna.
The time is in the early 1930's.

ACT I:  In and around a small village in the late Spring.
ACT II:  Two days later.

Setting Design by Bob Beaver & Cindy-Ann Burt Fronhofer
Organ music composed & arranged by Charles Murn

# ACT I

*(SETTING: The stage is divided into three areas. The largest
is the laboratory which is Right. It should be higher than
the other areas as there is constant talk of it being on a
hill and also characters are always talking of it being
"up there" and looking up. It is an abandoned mill so
should be either wooden or perhaps stone. There are two
doors, one DR which has a small opening in it at eye
height and is only used once, and a door ULC which
ostensibly leads down stairs to the outside. A tall thin
window is UC. The set is dominated by an operating
table C which may or may not be on a small platform.
Above the door R there is a small alcove with a built in
bench and above it a series of panels, lights, switches and
whatever is available to be used for the "coming to life"
scene. A small table with a silver tray of instruments is
LC. The left wall is imaginary. There is a large operating
lamp hanging above the table. The set gives off a
mysterious air of darkened corners and shadows
everywhere. The stage Left area is the living room of the
Frankenstein house and is pleasant and warm. There is
a pair of French doors open UC which lead to a garden
and an archway DL leading to the rest of the house. The
only furniture necessary is a loveseat Left of Center and
a comfortable chair R with a table in front of it for tea.
Since this should be a cozy sitting room, any decor is
friendly and shows great taste and wealth. The third area*

*is DL and is small and used for many interim scenes hence it is black and is lit only to show the center of it for whatever small scene happens there.)*

*(Since the play takes place in the 1930's and in Central Europe the attitudes and bodywork of the actors must show this rather formal atmosphere. It is most important that the play flows from scene to scene with no stops as it builds to each climax. If music is used it should come in under the end of a scene and at the beginning of the next. Organ music is most appropriate but is not necessary as the play can unfold quickly without it and the suspense will build equally as well. It is most important that the actors play it seriously and with intensity. There are laughs already built into the script and the different audiences will all add their own laughter and screams as the story unfolds.)*

*(If there is music, it fades and there is a flash of lightning and a screaming wail is heard. Lights dim up DL where we see a rather hand-made coffin open. Beside it is the weeping and distraught MOTHER. The DAUGHTER enters either down the theatre aisle if this is used or from DL.)*

DAUGHTER: *(As she enters)* Mother! Mother!

MOTHER: *(Weeping on coffin)* My son. My son, dead.

DAUGHTER: *(She is in her late teens and the mother is appropriately older. Both are dressed in poor peasant garb)* Mother, please. It is over. He is gone.

*(Goes to her and comforts her.)*

MOTHER: I won't believe it! I cannot believe it! My boy!

DAUGHTER: *(Lifts her mother)* Come home, Mother. The funeral is over. The mourners have left. There is nothing here.

MOTHER: My son, your brother is here.

DAUGHTER: Not really, Mother. Only his body is here, just his body.

MOTHER: *(Brightens slightly)* Yes, yes, you are right, dear. Only his body is here. The boy we knew, he is elsewhere' in other hands.

DAUGHTER: Yes, Mother. Come, let us go home.

MOTHER: *(As they start off Right or down the theatre aisle if it is used)* He was a good boy, wasn't he? No matter what they say, we know he was a good boy.

DAUGHTER: Yes, we know.

MOTHER: *(One final look back at the coffin)* Goodbye, my boy, my own son.

DAUGHTER: Come, Mother. Leave him to others now, leave him to death. You must return to life.

MOTHER: He was a good boy, a good boy.

DAUGHTER: Yes, Mother.

*(They are off and we see two GRAVE DIGGERS DR in the inset. They are both dressed in work clothes with caps and the first one carries a shovel. They are middle-aged and obviously local.)*

FIRST: Crazy old woman.

SECOND: Grief clouds the mind, don't it?

FIRST: Good boy indeed. *(Looks into coffin)* Trouble,

that one, always caused trouble.

SECOND: *(Looks down at body)* You was no good. No conscience, that was your trouble. Did what you wanted and the devil take the hindmost.

FIRST: His poor mother. Did you hear her carryin' on? She thought he was good'un.

SECOND: *(Leans over coffin and talks to the body)* You fooled her, didn't you, boy, but no one else. We all know you was a bad'un. A big overgrown bully. Now it's time to close you up forever.

FIRST: *(As closes the lid)* Maybe you're better off where you are now.

SECOND: Come on, let's cover him up and get down to the pub for a pint before it closes.

FIRST: I'm with you.


*(From audience left aisle or from DL, in the inset we see VICTOR FRANKENSTEIN and his assistant, GORGO. VICTOR is about 30 years old and a good looking man but he tends to be excitable and extremely nervous when under strain. GORGO is a small, local peasant who has been shunned most of his life due to the fact that he is slightly hunched and has one leg shorter than the other. He is very eager to help VICTOR and would do anything for him. He carries a small doctor's bag.)*


VICTOR: *(From off stage)* Hold it there, men.

FIRST: What? Who's there?

SECOND: *(Shielding his eyes)* I can't see. Who are you?

VICTOR: *(Coming into view)* Just two mourners. We were delayed by the weather. We were too late for the funeral.

FIRST: It's been a bad night. There's strange currents in the air.

GORGO: *(Talks in a raspy whisper)* I don't like it. I don't want to be here. We should go, Master.

VICTOR: Quiet, Gorgo. Our place is here.

GORGO: *(Immediately obeying)* Yes, Master.

VICTOR: *(To GRAVE DIGGERS)* I heard you mention ale, did I not?

SECOND: Yes, sir, as soon as this here coffin is in the ground.

FIRST: 'Tis the third grave we've dug this night without stoppin'.

VICTOR: My friend here –

GORGO: Yes, yes, me. I am his friend.

VICTOR: – and I would appreciate a few minutes beside the coffin by ourselves, a few moments to say farewell to a companion. Suppose I give you this *(Takes money from his pocket)* and you go have your pint of ale and leave us to our grief. Give us but a few minutes and then you can resume your work.

FIRST: Well, I don't know –

SECOND: We *have* worked hard for several hours.

GORGO: And our companion will not leave, will he?

*(Snickers at his own joke.)*

VICTOR: No, he will be here when you return.

FIRST: I suppose it's all right. No harm done to wait a half hour, is there?

SECOND: No harm at all.

VICTOR: Here. *(Hands him the money)* Leave us to our grief.

GORGO: Yes, our grief.

*(Pulls out a kerchief.)*

FIRST: *(Takes money)* Thank you, sir. This will be our little secret, won't it?

VICTOR: Yes, indeed. Go have a few minutes rest over a pint. Leave us with our friend.

SECOND: *(As they start to exit DR)* Thank you, sir. We sure appreciate this.

FIRST: Yes, Herr – your name sir? Did you say?

VICTOR: No, I did not. Names are not important at times like this.

FIRST: No, sir.

VICTOR: *(Suddenly very strong and authoritative)* Go, please. Leave us.

FIRST: Yes sir.

*(They scurry out DR or up the aisle.)*

SECOND: *(In a whisper as they exit)* Here's a bit of luck on a dreary night.

FIRST: Generous man. We can have more than one pint.

SECOND: I hope the body will wait for us.

FIRST: Of course. Where is he going anyway?

VICTOR: *(Looking after them)* Where indeed, eh, Gorgo?

GORGO: They don't know, do they, Master?

VICTOR: No. No one knows.

GORGO: They don't even suspect that you are Victor Frankenstein.

VICTOR: Quiet, Gorgo! Soon the world will know Victor Frankenstein not as just another scientist but as the one who pierced the barriers which have existed since time began.

GORGO: *(Opens coffin lid)* And you, you don't know what awaits you. You don't know what my master can do.

VICTOR: We are going to do what no one has ever done since the first small creature crawled out of the sea. We are going to create life – create life from death, reverse the very meaning of existence.

GORGO: Yes, Master.

VICTOR: This was a decent man here, a strong man with a good brain. This is the last piece of our puzzle, Gorgo. The rest of the body we pieced together is ready to receive this brain. Let us get started. Give me the bag.

GORGO: *(Hands him the doctor's bag)* Here, Master. *(Looks out over audience)* I will make sure no one comes, no one sees.

VICTOR: *(Opens bag and takes out a cloth which he lays over the coffin edge and also a scalpel or large knife)* Yes, keep your eyes open, Gorgo. We are getting close to the end of our experiment, close to the end of the beginning.

GORGO: Yes, Master.

VICTOR: Now for the brain that will send new life through a body which has never existed.

GORGO: Hurry, Master. Hurry.

VICTOR: Now we start. *(Music in and under if used. VICTOR holds the knife)* This is the moment I have waited for and worked for. Now, I take the brain!

*(Raises the knife as blackout.)*

*(Lights come up on FRANKENSTEIN's living room as BERTA enters carrying a tea tray which holds tea pot, sugar, creamer, 2 cups, saucers and spoons, and a small plate of tea sandwiches. BERTA is a young, local girl who is delighted to be working in the Manor House and does her best to please but she is a trifle over-anxious. She puts the tray on the table below the chair. She goes to the French doors to look out as FREDERICA enters. She is middle-aged or older and the current head of the household. She is a warm and loving motherly type of woman.)*

FREDERICA: Berta, I see tea is ready.

BERTA: Yes, Ma'am.

FREDERICA: And Elizabeth, is she out there in the garden?

BERTA: Yes, Ma'am.

FREDERICA: *(As she sits by the tea and starts to pour)* Will you call her in, please.

BERTA: Yes, Ma'am. *(Calls in a very loud voice out the doors)* Miss Elizabeth!

FREDERICA: Quietly, Berta, quietly.

BERTA: How can I call quietly?

FREDERICA: They don't need to hear you in Vienna.

BERTA: I'll try to call quietly.

*(Opens her mouth to call just as ELIZABETH answers from off stage.)*

ELIZABETH: Yes, Berta.

BERTA: *(To FREDERICA)* See, Miss Frederica, she heard me right enough.

FREDERICA: Never mind, Berta. Tell her tea is ready.

BERTA: *(Calls again in a loud voice)* Tea is –

FREDERICA: Berta –

BERTA: *(In a whisper)* – ready, Miss Elizabeth.

FREDERICA: Much better, dear.

ELIZABETH: *(Enters from the garden through the door. She is a lovely young woman, bright and happy but there is definite strength within her)* Berta, you have such a lovely, clear voice. Thank you for calling me.

BERTA: *(Curtsies)* Thank you, Miss.

ELIZABETH: *(Crossing to tea table)* I'm just in the mood for tea.

FREDERICA: And some nice little sandwiches.

BERTA: Cook made them. They're delicious.

ELIZABETH: *(Teasing her)* How do you know, Berta?

BERTA: Well, I –

ELIZABETH: *(Picks up the sandwich plate)* There seems to be an empty space where one sandwich recently resided.

BERTA: *(Comes and bends over the plate, all innocence)* Really?

ELIZABETH: Right there. I expect it fell onto the floor in the hallway.

BERTA: Yes, yes it did.

ELIZABETH: And you didn't want to put it back on the plate, did you?

BERTA: No, no, I didn't.

ELIZABETH: So you did something else with it?

BERTA: I – I –

ELIZABETH: But we don't want to know what happened to it, do we, Aunt Frederica?

FREDERICA: *(Trying not to smile)* No, no, we don't.

BERTA: *(Not realizing she is saying it)* Good.

FREDERICA: That will be all, Berta, thank you.

BERTA: *(Scurries out quickly)* Yes, Ma'am.

FREDERICA: *(Laughs along with ELIZABETH)* I shall never get that child trained properly.

ELIZABETH: It would be such a pity if she were. There is something rather charming about her innocence, don't you think?

FREDERICA: Charming but tiring.

*(Hands tea to ELIZABETH.)*

ELIZABETH: I've always thought it so nice of you and Uncle to employ so many of the townspeople here and on the farmlands. They're very loyal to you and well they should be.

*(Sits on the sofa.)*

FREDERICA: Oh, piffle, it's nothing.

ELIZABETH: And how grateful they are as we all are, especially me.

FREDERICA: Oh, now, Elizabeth, you have brought such joy into our lives. When I came here to live with my brother, I thought I would end up the usual maiden aunt taking care of and being taken care of but then my brother took you on as his ward and you brought sunshine into this house.

ELIZABETH: You embarrass me.

FREDERICA: Now with my brother gone and I, myself, in charge of everything I realize how strange life can treat one.

ELIZABETH: *(Puts her cup on the table above the sofa and crosses to FREDERICA)* I shall always look upon you as the mother I never knew.

FREDERICA: And when your marriage takes place, I –

ELIZABETH: *(Crosses above her)* Now, none of that, Aunt. You shall stay here after Victor and I are married. You are part of the family. This is your home as much as mine and I know Victor agrees.

FREDERICA: I had always hoped, as had my brother, that you and Victor would join in matrimony but I want to be sure it is how you feel.

ELIZABETH: *(Crosses to window)* Of course it is, you know it is. We have been destined for this wedding since our first meeting when he was ten and I was three and he threw me into that mud puddle ... I knew it was naught but love.

FREDERICA: But I have often wondered –

ELIZABETH: *(Turns)* What? Wondered what?

FREDERICA: If perhaps Henry ... I mean you three, when you were young ... and then he went off to University and ... oh, never mind. I shouldn't have brought this up except I just wondered –

ELIZABETH: *(Goes to her)* Aunt Frederica, you are so subtle.

FREDERICA: Am I?

ELIZABETH: Yes, I believe Henry was – what term should I use? – infatuated with me. Does that sound conceited?

FREDERICA: No, dear, just truthful.

ELIZABETH: *(Picks up her cup and crosses to tray and picks up a sandwich)* We three grew up together with him living so close by, but then he went off for those years of study and when he returned it was as though we were meeting for the first time.

FREDERICA: And you being young and pretty –

ELIZABETH: – and available –

FREDERICA: – made you even more desirable. I see.

ELIZABETH: Yes, Henry will always be our best friend. I know he will.

FREDERICA: And your feelings for him?

ELIZABETH: That of a very good friend. *(Goes to doors, quickly interrupting the conversation)* I wish Victor would come back, perhaps for dinner. Do you think so?

FREDERICA: *(Goes to her at the doors)* He has spent so much time up there.

ELIZABETH: *(They are both looking out the windows towards R)* Why can he not have his laboratory here in the house, in the East wing for instance, but, no, he has to have it way up there atop that mountain.

FREDERICA: And the way the townspeople talk of the wagon loads of equipment that are hauled up there almost daily. What does it all mean?

ELIZABETH: *(Turns to her)* I don't know but Victor says when this experiment, as he calls it, is completed he will be famous, the world will be at our feet. I don't want the world, Aunt. I only want a marriage, a home, and children.

FREDERICA: I know my dear.

ELIZABETH: He has changed so of late. What do you think is really going on up there?

FREDERICA: I don't know.

ELIZABETH: In some ways I don't want to know, yet I feel I must find out. *(Turns and looks toward the laboratory)* Oh, Victor, what experiment are you doing way up there in that laboratory?

*(They are both looking out the windows towards the laboratory as the music comes in if used and lights come up on the laboratory. ELIZABETH and FREDERICA exit in the dark. If a scrim is used to cover the laboratory it is now pulled back. The focus of attention is always on the operating table where a body is now lying covered by a sheet. This is either the actor who plays the CREATURE or a dummy used until the "coming to life" scene. Over the table there is a large cone suspended with various bulbs both inside and outside which will be used to full effect later on. If a dummy is used now rather than the actor then a large, folding "protective" screen should be placed around the table so the actor can come on-stage later without being seen by the audience. If the screen is used then VICTOR removes it at the beginning of this scene and stores it aside till it is used again later. As the lights come up VICTOR is seen with stethoscope in hand leaning over and above the body.)*

VICTOR: *(Calls)* Gorgo! Gorgo, hurry man! Hurry!

GORGO: *(Off stage UC)* Coming, Master, coming.

VICTOR: Quickly before it is late.

GORGO: *(Enters UC carrying something wrapped in a cloth)* Here it is, Master.

VICTOR: Quickly.

GORGO: It is still cold from the cellar.

VICTOR: Good.

GORGO: Cold and damp.

VICTOR: Let me see.

GORGO: Here. It is perfect.

*(Shows him what is wrapped up. It is a hand with the stump
    of the wrist showing.)*

VICTOR: *(Holds it)* Yes, cold now as it should be.

GORGO: But soon it will be warm.

VICTOR: When the blood courses through it then it will
move again and you can even shake hands with it, Gorgo.

GORGO: Yes, yes. You put pieces together and you
make me a friend. I will soon shake hands with my friend.

VICTOR: The tray. Hand me the tray.

GORGO: Yes, Master.

*(Hands him the silver tray of instruments from the table L.)*

VICTOR: *(Lifts part of the sheet)* Yes, the wrist is ready.
It is better than before.

GORGO: The first hand we had. No good?

VICTOR: It wouldn't have worked but this one, this one
is going to be perfect. It is the correct size and will fuse
properly.

GORGO: Then we bring my friend to life?

VICTOR: Once this is in place then all we have to do is
wait for a storm and we will implant the brain just before the
heavens open up.

GORGO: Lightning. Much lightning.

VICTOR: *(He has been choosing instruments to use)* As
much as the heavens can send down. We must have electricity
– electricity most powerful.

GORGO: Then life, and I have a friend.

VICTOR: *(Moves L of table)* Then the world will know
what we have done. Old Dr. Hellstrom in Vienna will want

me to write papers on this. They will be sorry they sent me packing from University. They will want to make me a professor but I shall refuse. That will be my ultimate triumph but I shall refuse. *(He has worked himself up and we start to see the depth of his intensity as he continues to work.) (There is a loud sound of a large knocker on what is assumed to be the downstairs door.)* What is that?

GORGO: *(Goes to window and looks down)* The door. Someone is there.

VICTOR: No! No one must come here!

GORGO: Is it more equipment?

VICTOR: We need no more. We are complete.

GORGO: Yes, someone is there. It is two people.

VICTOR: Not now. I must finish this.

GORGO: *(Yelling down through the window)* Away! Go away! Get out!

ELIZABETH: *(At a distance from below)* Victor. Victor, are you there? It's Elizabeth.

GORGO: Go away!

VICTOR: *(Goes to window. He is getting frantic)* Elizabeth –

ELIZABETH: *(Off stage)* I'm here with Aunt Frederica. We came by carriage. We –

VICTOR: Elizabeth, I told you not to come here.

FREDERICA: *(Off stage)* Victor, please, we are worried about you.

ELIZABETH: *(Off stage)* Are you ill? We have not seen you in so long.

VICTOR: I am fine. My experiment is almost finished.

ELIZABETH: *(Off stage)* What is it? What are you doing, Victor?

GORGO: *(Whispers)* Send them away. They must go away.

VICTOR: I will be home shortly.

FREDERICA: *(Off stage)* Can't we come in? Can't we see what you are doing?

ELIZABETH: *(Off stage)* Yes, Victor, let us in. Please.

VICTOR: No! No!

GORGO: *(Whispers)* Not in here, never in here.

ELIZABETH: *(Off stage)* We are coming in.

VICTOR: The door is bolted! Go! Go away!

ELIZABETH: *(Off stage. Shocked)* Victor!

VICTOR: In the name of God, go!

*(Returns to table and operation.)*

ELIZABETH: *(Off stage with more pounding on door)* Victor!

VICTOR: Here, Gorgo, stand by me.

GORGO: Yes, Master.

*(Goes to him.)*

VICTOR: Damn women should stay where they belong. Interfering with this. They have no right.

GORGO: *(Goes back to window)* They are leaving, Master. The carriage is going down the hill.

VICTOR: Good.

GORGO: You told them, Master.

VICTOR: I fear I was too strong but they must understand. Elizabeth is to be my wife. She must be made to understand.

GORGO: When she sees my friend here she will understand.

*(Pats the body during the above.)*

VICTOR: Then the world will understand.

GORGO: When my friend gets his brain –

VICTOR: The brain! It must remain in tact. It must not deteriorate.

GORGO: *(Gets the covered brain jar from table and hands it to VICTOR)* It is perfect.

VICTOR: *(Whips off the cloth to show the brain in a glass jar. The jar can contain dry ice which gives a smoldering effect or plain Jell-O which is also effective)* There it is, the final piece in our puzzle. Still as good as the day we got it, Gorgo. A brain from an intelligent human being.

GORGO: And soon the brain of my friend.

VICTOR: The storm. When the storm comes then this will be implanted and he will live.

GORGO: My friend will live.

VICTOR: This body will live. I will have created life. *(Holds up brain and faces front)* I will have gone beyond mankind's bounds. I shall step into the infinite mystery of life.

*(Blackout and music if used. Lights come up on the living room where ELIZABETH is sitting in the chair R and embroidering. A basket is beside her.)*

BERTA: *(Rushes in excitedly)* Miss Elizabeth. Miss Elizabeth.

ELIZABETH: Yes, Berta.

BERTA: Oh, Miss Elizabeth.

ELIZABETH: Either the house is afire or Aunt Frederica has given you a holiday. Such excitement.

BERTA: Yes, Ma'am.

ELIZABETH: Now calm down and tell me what it is.

BERTA: It is a gentleman, Miss.

ELIZABETH: Is that so extraordinary?

BERTA: This one is, Miss.

ELIZABETH: What is he, tall, short, green, blue, or what?

BERTA: No, just a gentleman.

ELIZABETH: I see what you mean, Berta, a gentleman that you would like to go walking out with. Is that what you mean?

BERTA: Oh, yes, Miss.

ELIZABETH: *(Enjoying all this)* Did he ask you?

BERTA: *(Blushing)* Oh, no, Miss, he is a gentleman.

ELIZABETH: Who do you usually go out walking with, Berta, if not a gentleman.

BERTA: I mean a *real* gentleman, this one is. I mean – oh, Miss, you confuse me.

ELIZABETH: Do you suppose this gentleman is still standing in the hallway or has he left by now?

BERTA: I hope not. Oh, his card.

*(Hands ELIZABETH his calling card.)*

ELIZABETH: *(Reads it)* It's Henry. *(Puts knitting away in basket)* Good heavens, Girl, it's our dearest friend, Henry Lovitz. Show him in at once.

BERTA: Yes, Miss, with great pleasure.

*(Scurries out.)*

ELIZABETH: *(Tidies herself and rises)* Henry, Henry, where are you?

HENRY: *(Enters. HENRY is a very good looking, pleasant man who has always been in love with ELIZABETH and will protect her at all costs. He goes to her)* Elizabeth.

ELIZABETH: Henry, what a delightful surprise.

*(Kisses him on both cheeks.)*

HENRY: *(Takes both her hands)* Let me look at you.

ELIZABETH: Come now, you have been among all those beautiful city creatures in their finery.

HENRY: But no one can compare with dear Elizabeth.

ELIZABETH: *(Moves away R)* Did you come here to embarrass me?

HENRY: No.

ELIZABETH: *(Turns with a smile)* Because I love it. Tell me more.

HENRY: You'll become too conceited.

ELIZABETH: *(Takes his hand, leads him to the sofa and they sit)* Then tell me everything that's happened. Your work since the University in Estate Management, has it been rewarding?

HENRY: Very, and soon I shall return here for good and tend to my family's holdings.

ELIZABETH: It will be so wonderful, we three together again just as if we had never grown up and separated.

HENRY: How is Victor? Is he here?

ELIZABETH: No, he's at his laboratory.

HENRY: Yes, I heard he has turned that old, falling apart mill into his work space.

ELIZABETH: *(Goes to windows and looks out towards UR)* You can see it from here.

HENRY: *(Joins her)* And that is where he is working on his mysterious experiments?

ELIZABETH: You know about them?

HENRY: A bit from his letters which have not been overly informative. I thought perhaps you knew more.

ELIZABETH: *(Crosses away down and right)* I know nothing of his work. He doesn't confide in me. He is becoming a stranger. Oh, Henry, I am so worried.

HENRY: *(Goes to her)* But everything is all right between you two, isn't it? The marriage, is it still going to take place?

ELIZABETH: *(Crosses away below sofa)* Yes, of course ... in due time.

HENRY: But I thought it was to be this Spring.

ELIZABETH: And so it was but it seems experiments have taken precedence.

HENRY: Over your marriage? I don't believe this of Victor.

ELIZABETH: *(Sits upstage end of sofa)* Henry, you don't understand.

HENRY: *(Goes to her)* I understand that we have both been in love with you since the day we first met –

ELIZABETH: *(Turns away)* Henry, don't –

HENRY: *(Circles around sofa and sits)* Victor won your heart, that I know, and I stepped aside as best I could but now

– what is he thinking to postpone your wedding?

ELIZABETH: Henry, we three have been as close as any people could be, you know that. We have known since the beginning that Victor and I were betrothed so we have ignored any other feelings which might have grown during the years. Let us leave it that way, please, dear Henry.

HENRY: As you wish, but let me just say that if ever Victor mistreats you or your feelings for him alter, I –

ELIZABETH: *(Puts her fingers on his lips)* I know. I know.

FREDERICA: *(As she comes through the windows)* Henry Lovitz. I heard you were here.

HENRY: *(Rises and goes to her)* Aunt Frederica. May I still call you that?

FREDERICA: *(Gives him a small kiss)* Of course. Berta said there was a dashing gentleman in here and that Elizabeth seemed all atwitter so I knew it was no one but Henry Lovitz. Will you take tea with us? I will call Berta.

HENRY: I was about to ask Elizabeth to go into the village with me. There is someone there I would like her to meet.

ELIZABETH: Here in our village? Someone visiting?

HENRY: A vacationer who may be able to shed some light on this change in Victor.

FREDERICA: *(Her worry and concern showing)* Did Elizabeth tell you we went to his laboratory the other day and he would not give us entry? He raised his voice. He ordered us to leave.

HENRY: What has changed him so? Is he ill?

ELIZABETH: He said he was well but so very busy with whatever this experiment is.

FREDERICA: He has been staying up there for days at a time with his assistant.

HENRY: Who is that?

FREDERICA: *(Moves below chair)* We have never met, we've only seen him from a distance. Victor rarely comes home and when he does he is so preoccupied we can hardly talk to him.

ELIZABETH: He looks at me but I know what he is seeing is elsewhere. He almost frightens me, Henry.

FREDERICA: *(Sits in the chair)* It has been getting worse and worse.

ELIZABETH: Ever since he left the University and worked by himself in Vienna he has been getting less and less communicative.

HENRY: *(Moves above sofa)* He told you he left the University those three years ago?

ELIZABETH: That is what he led us to believe.

HENRY: He was asked to leave.

FREDERICA: That couldn't be. He was graduated with honors and his research was going so well.

HENRY: The Dean of Science Professors, Dr. Hellstrom, talked to me about Victor, that he is potentially the greatest scientist in Europe today.

ELIZABETH: Potentially?

HENRY: But instead of continuing his research he went off on his own delving into fields of experimentation he was not yet ready to explore.

FREDERICA: But surely he knows what he is doing?

HENRY: *(Goes below sofa to her)* Does he? That is the question in my mind and also in Dr. Hellstrom's.

ELIZABETH: You think Victor might harm himself?

HENRY: I told you there was someone I wanted you to meet, Elizabeth.

ELIZABETH: Yes.

HENRY: It is the very Dr. Hellstrom.

ELIZABETH: Here in our village?

HENRY: He is on vacation and I begged him to stop off at the hotel on his way to Val D'Isere. Victor respects him so and I thought if the Doctor talked to him he might find out what is going on.

ELIZABETH: *(Rises and goes to him)* You think Victor will see this Dr. Hellstrom and perhaps even let him into his laboratory?

HENRY: He was his professor. I am sure he will see him.

BERTA: *(In archway)* Excuse me. Ma'am. Should I bring in tea for you and the nice gentleman?

*(She gives a huge smile to HENRY.)*

FREDERICA: For me, Berta, please, but I believe Miss Elizabeth and "the nice gentleman" are going into the hotel for theirs.

BERTA: That's too bad. I mean, Yes, Ma'am. Shall I bring in a cup for Mr. Victor?

ELIZABETH: Victor? He's not here.

BERTA: Yes, Miss. He's rummaging about a bit upstairs. Didn't you hear him come in?

ELIZABETH: No, we didn't.

FREDERICA: Yes, Berta, bring an extra cup. In fact, bring enough for all of us. Perhaps Victor will stay awhile and we can catch up on things.

BERTA: Yes. Ma'am.

*(Exits)*

FREDERICA: *(Rises)* This is a Godsend. Perhaps, Henry, you can make sense of what is going on, of what has changed Victor.

HENRY: I shall certainly try.

VICTOR: *(Off stage)* No, Berta, no tea. I cannot stay.

BERTA: *(Off stage as ELIZABETH sits on the sofa trying to calm herself)* But they're in there. Mr. Victor, with a new gentleman, a nice gentleman, a Mr. Lovitz.

VICTOR: *(Off stage)* Henry? Henry here?

BERTA: *(Off stage)* Yes, sir.

VICTOR: *(Comes rushing in from left. He is very agitated in this scene)* Henry, where are you?

HENRY: Victor, so good to see you.

VICTOR: *(As they shake hands)* My good friend, Henry. I'm so delighted. Elizabeth, is this not a happy surprise?

ELIZABETH: Yes, indeed.

FREDERICA: *(Sits in the chair)* Sit down, Victor, and join us for tea. We have seen so little of you lately.

VICTOR: No, no, I can't stay. I mustn't.

HENRY: Surely for a few minutes.

VICTOR: Any other time but not tonight.

ELIZABETH: What is tonight?

VICTOR: Tonight there is to be a storm.

FREDERICA: Yes, I heard, a severe electrical storm.

VICTOR: The grandfather of all storms.

FREDERICA: Then why go back up the mountain to your laboratory? Stay here with us.

VICTOR: *(Goes to windows. HENRY follows him)* No, tonight is the climax of my experiment. Tonight history will be made up there. After tonight life as we know it will be thought of quite differently.

HENRY: Victor, what is this experiment? Tell me, please. You make it sound so exciting.

VICTOR: It is beyond exciting. It is daring to cross into the absolute unknown.

HENRY: Let me come. Let me be with you for this.

VICTOR: *(Losing his temper, he becomes very loud and we start to see the more neurotic side of VICTOR)* No! No one must be there. I have my assistant. I have all I need.

HENRY: I, too, could help.

VICTOR: No! Let me alone, all of you! This is the night I have waited and worked for but I must be alone. Alone!

*(He bursts out the windows.)*

ELIZABETH: *(In tears, she takes a handkerchief she has in her sleeve)* Victor! Victor, what has happened to you?

FREDERICA: *(Rises)* Please, Elizabeth, you mustn't cry.

HENRY: *(Goes to ELIZABETH)* Elizabeth, go into the village and meet this Dr. Hellstrom.

ELIZABETH: Yes, yes –

FREDERICA: Perhaps he can help.

HENRY: Yes. If the climax of the experiment is to be tonight we must act quickly. Dr. Hellstrom will know what to do. Come, Elizabeth, we must make haste.

FREDERICA: Thank God you are here, Henry.

HENRY: If Vienna we use automobiles but here I have a carriage waiting outside.

ELIZABETH: I'm ready, Henry. Let us hurry.

*(They are off.)*

FREDERICA: *(Runs to the windows. To herself)* Victor, Victor, be careful.

BERTA: *(Enters)* I have the tea all ready in the kitchen but everyone seems to have gone except you.

FREDERICA: Yes, Berta, just bring one cup for me.

BERTA: Yes Ma'am. *(Starts to leave and turns back)* Oh, Miss Frederica, I'm not goin' out tonight even if it is me evenin' off.

FREDERICA: Really?

BERTA: Yes. They say there is going to be a big storm, a great electric storm and I'm frightened.

*(Exits)*

FREDERICA: *(Left alone, she looks out windows towards the laboratory)* Yes, the grandfather of all storms.

*(Music comes in and Blackout. Lights cross-fade to the laboratory. During this scene we hear thunder in the distance and occasional lightning which is not as bright as in later scenes. GORGO is standing above the body which is still draped. He lifts the edge of the sheet and takes out an arm with the hand now attached with some stitches showing.)*

GORGO: My friend. You will be my friend, won't you? Soon you will live. The great storm is due tonight. It will bring blood flowing through your veins and you will live. I will have a friend I can be proud of. All my life people have turned away from me because I am not like them but now I will show them. I will have a friend who is like them – tall and perfect and all eyes will turn when I walk down street with you, my new friend.

*(He pats the hand as VICTOR comes in UC in a high state of excitement.)*

VICTOR: Gorgo! Don't touch him!

GORGO: He is my friend.

VICTOR: *(Puts hand back under sheet)* Tonight he will be your friend if you wish but now it is just skin and bone, muscle and sinew which I have put together into one body.

GORGO: Tonight. Yes, tonight. *(Goes to window as we see there is thunder and lightning in the distance)* The sky darkens. The storm is coming.

VICTOR: The storm we have waited for.

GORGO: Hurry, Master, the last part. When do you put in the last part?

VICTOR: Now, Gorgo, now is the time for the brain.

GORGO: *(Gets brain from table L)* Here, Master. Here is the brain.

VICTOR: *(Holds the jar)* This is the very center of my new being, the core of its thinking and behavior. It belonged to a good, decent man. We know that, don't we, Gorgo?

GORGO: Yes, Master, the mother said so.

VICTOR: Cut short in life too soon but now to live again. The instruments, uncover the instruments.

*(VICTOR puts on rubber gloves.)*

GORGO: *(Uncovers instruments and brings them to VICTOR)* Here they are, Master, clean and shining for your clever fingers.

VICTOR: *(Holds our a slightly shaking hand)* Shaking. My hand must not shake. One small mistake and all is lost. I must be calm. Everything depends on the next few moments. The brain must be in place by the time the storm breaks. *(Picks up scalpel)* Now, Gorgo, now I am ready.

GORGO: Yes, Master. I shall pray for you and for him.

VICTOR: Pray? Dare we pray?

GORGO: Whatever you say, Master.

VICTOR: I think not. We are going into a nether world where prayer is unknown.

GORGO: Master, you frighten me.

VICTOR: We are both frightened but is not fear normal? *(Lifts part of sheet and ostensibly makes a cut)* I have made the first cut. We have begun. Hand me the retractor.

GORGO: Yes, Master.

VICTOR: We have started. Now there is no turning back.

*(Thunder and lightening. Blackout and lights come up DL in the corner of the hotel. There is a table with three straight chairs around it. Perhaps a potted plant is in one corner but no set it needed. DR. HELLSTROM is seated above the table. He is a gray-haired and kindly looking man but one is aware of his authority. ELIZABETH, in hat, jacket, and with a reticule, is seated to the R of the table and HENRY to the L. Tea cups are in front of them. They are in mid-conversation.)*

HENRY: ... but, Dr. Hellstrom, Victor is such a brilliant

scientist. Why did the University not let him continue his research?

HELLSTROM: He was beginning to tell the instructors what they should do, what experiments they should make.

ELIZABETH: Tact has never been Victor's strong suit.

HELLSTROM: He began not showing up for the lectures and spending more and more time in the laboratory.

HENRY: With his mind, isn't that to be expected?

HELLSTROM: Yes, but he began demanding more and more specimens to work on.

HENRY: The University always had an ample supply.

HELLSTROM: But he wanted not only the cadavers we had on hand but more fresh ones. *(ELIZABETH gives a small gasp)* Forgive me, Miss. We scientists are used to such talk.

ELIZABETH: I understand. Please continue.

HELLSTROM: I should not say this as I have no proof but – *(Looks about to be sure he is not overheard)* after Victor and the University parted company there was a rash of burglaries.

ELIZABETH: But surely not Victor. That's ridiculous, a member of the House of Frankenstein a thief?

HENRY: Elizabeth, I believe Dr. Hellstrom is not alluding to common burglary, are you, Doctor?

HELLSTROM: Henry is right. I refer to the appearance of a ghoul.

ELIZABETH: A grave robber? You can't think –

HELLSTROM: As I said, there as no proof but from what Victor has told colleagues he was never at a loss for cadavers.

ELIZABETH: This is all too horrible to believe.

HENRY: *(Rises)* Elizabeth, let me take you home. Doctor, please wait here for me.

ELIZABETH: No, please, Henry. I must know what is going on. We must face the truth, however ugly it may be.

HENRY: *(Sits again)* As you wish.

ELIZABETH: *(After a tentative start)* There is something neither of you know and I am hesitant to mention it.

HENRY: What is it?

ELIZABETH: It may be of no importance. I hope it is only coincidence but –

HENRY: Yes.

ELIZABETH: Just days before you returned, Henry, there was a robbery in the next village – in the cemetery.

HELLSTROM: A body was stolen?

ELIZABETH: It seems the mourners had left and the grave diggers were about to bury the – person, but two men appeared. They said they were friends of the deceased and they sent the grave diggers off to the local pub while they ostensibly had a few minutes alone to mourn.

HENRY: Two men you say?

ELIZABETH: Yes. When the grave diggers returned in a half hour they found ...

HENRY: Yes, yes ...

ELIZABETH: I can hardly say the words.

HELLSTROM: Come, my dear, you must. What did they find?

ELIZABETH: The body had been desecrated. The head had been removed and was lying beside the coffin and – and ...

HENRY: Yes –

ELIZABETH: *(Almost in a faint)* – it was split open and the brain removed.

*(She takes a bottle of smelling salts from her reticule. HENRY goes to her and holds the bottle for her to breathe.)*

HENRY: Here, let me help you. Take a few breaths. This will soon pass.

HELLSTROM: A brain. A brain is missing? Two men. You say Victor has an assistant?

HENRY: So it seems.

HELLSTROM: And his preoccupation with mastering the line between life and death, does this mean he will try – the storm. You said he spoke of a huge storm.

HENRY: He said it is necessary to his experiment.

HELLSTROM: He was always so sure there was a connection between life and electricity. Do you think – might he – ?

HENRY: Tonight. The storm is tonight. What has he planned?

HELLSTROM: *(Rises)* We must go. We must go to his laboratory at once.

HENRY: *(Moves R)* Elizabeth, I will send you home in a carriage.

ELIZABETH: No. I will come. I must be with you. Don't you see, I must know. *(Rises and goes to HENRY)* Henry, you of all people know how important it is for me – for us.

HENRY: Yes, I do.

HELLSTROM: Come, there is not a minute to lose.

ELIZABETH: *(As they all look R towards the laboratory)* Henry, what will we find up there? What is Victor doing?

HENRY: We shall soon know.

ELIZABETH: I pray it will be all right.

HELLSTROM: Pray if you wish but I fear it may be too late for prayers. Come, hurry.

*(They exit as music in and lights fade to black. Thunder grows louder and lightning is seen flashing through the laboratory as VICTOR speaks.)*

VICTOR: The storm is about to break. Turn the lights back on, Gorgo.

GORGO: Yes, Master.

*(Lights up as he presses switch on panel. During the scene occasional lightning and thunder reoccur growing bigger all the time.)*

VICTOR: *(Crosses to body which remains under the sheet)* You are ready, aren't you? Your brain is in place. Everything is set. Now for the final test. Gorgo, stand back. I am going to throw the switch to make sure everything is set right.

GORGO: *(Moves away L)* Yes, Master.

VICTOR: One – two – three. *(Pulls one of the main switches on the panel and there is an effect which is not as large as it will be but gives an indication. The lights above and inside the cone above the table flicker and lights from above the room ostensibly outside the roof flicker. They finish as he shuts switch off)* Perfect. Everything is perfect.

GORGO: *(Rushes above the body)* My friend, soon you will awaken. Life will be wonderful for you.

VICTOR: Quickly, before the storm is at its height. The electrodes. The wires must be attached so the electricity will bring him to life.

*(Pulls wires with clamps attached from under the table and attaches them under the sheet.)*

GORGO: He will live, won't he, Master? Tell me my friend will come alive.

VICTOR: Yes, yes, of course. There, the wires are attaching smoothly. *(Looks up at the cone over the table which is hung to raise and lower)* Once the lightning comes down through this you will live, my creature, you will live for the first time.

*(Loud knocking on outside door downstage UC.)*

VICTOR: What is that?

GORGO: *(Goes to the window)* The door. Someone is there. Yes, three people are down there.

VICTOR: Send them away. No one must be here. We don't have any more time. We must start now. Send them away.

GORGO: *(As he rushes out UL)* Yes, Master.

VICTOR: *(Goes to panel of dials and switches R and checks them)* Check. One final check. Everything must be right. One small error and he will not live.

GORGO: *(Off stage)* No, no, away! Get away!

HENRY: *(Off stage)* We must come in.

GORGO: *(Off stage)* No! Master, they are forcing the door.

HENRY: *(Off stage)* We must see Dr. Frankenstein.

GORGO: *(Off stage)* No! No! Master, they are coming up!

VICTOR: *(As HENRY enters)* Henry, how dare you come in here?

HENRY: *(Goes to him at R)* Victor, we must know what is going on here.

VICTOR: No. None of your business. Get out!

HENRY: *(As HELLSTROM enters followed by ELIZABETH)* I have Dr. Hellstrom with me.

VICTOR: Hellstrom, what are you doing here?

HELLSTROM: I come as your teacher or perhaps as your pupil. We shall see.

HENRY: *(ELIZABETH comes in sight)* And Elizabeth.

*(She comes DC.)*

VICTOR: *(Goes to her)* Elizabeth, no. I beg of you, don't stay. Go home now before it is too late.

ELIZABETH: If this is so important to you then should I not share in it?

VICTOR: No! Get out, all of you!

HELLSTROM: As a scientist and your friend I must remain.

HENRY: We shall stay.

GORGO: *(Rushes in)* Master, the storm. It is at its height. We must not miss it.

VICTOR: And we shall not. *(GORGO watches the storm from the window. To others)* Very well, you have asked for it. Stay down over there. *(Indicates DR and they stand there, ELIZABETH down stage, HENRY above her and HELLSTROM above him as VICTOR checks props, dials, etc.)* Dr. Hellstrom you will be interested to know that during my experimentation in that laboratory outside Vienna I had a heart, a human heart. Don't ask me from whence it came. I was out of the room for an instant when that room was illuminated by lightning. I rushed in and the heart was beating. Beating, do you hear? Only for a few moments but I knew then that there is a connection between the greatest electricity we know and life itself. I continued on that theory and I arrived as this. *(Goes to the body)* It is a body put together from many other bodies. It has never lived before in this form but tonight you will see it breathe life. Just awhile ago I put the final element in place – the brain.

ELIZABETH: Oh, no.

*(The storm gradually heightens in intensity.)*

HELLSTROM: And where did you get this brain?

VICTOR: Does it matter?

GORGO: Master, hurry!

VICTOR: It is the brain of a decent man who died of natural causes.

ELIZABETH: If it was removed just before the body was buried a few days ago then it is the brain of a common criminal.

VICTOR: But the mother said he was a good man.

ELIZABETH: Of course, Victor, any mother would say the same of her son but this man was always in trouble. He was described as a man without a conscience.

HELLSTROM: *(Crosses into table)* That brain, you must not use it. If you are successful and the creature survives –

GORGO: *(Goes L of VICTOR)* He will. He is my friend.

VICTOR: It is too late. I must proceed now. The brain is in a different element. It can be trained.

HENRY: Think, Victor.

VICTOR: I am going ahead. Gorgo, get ready.

GORGO: Yes, Master.

VICTOR: Stay back, all of you. *(Note: If a shield is used insert the following dialogue to allow the CREATURE to get in place of the dummy. If the CREATURE is already in place ignore next speeches)* Gorgo, the shield.

GORGO: Yes, Master.

*(GORGO and VICTOR take the large screen and place it in front of the operating table. The CREATURE can come in through a cut-out in the US wall and remove the dummy through same cut-out. This can all be done during the pyrotechnics of coming alive.)*

VICTOR: This shield is used to protect you from any harmful rays. We are already immune to them. Keep well back.

GORGO: Master, we are ready. The storm is at its height.

VICTOR: This is it, this will be my triumph, I know it. One, two, three. *(He pulls the switches and all possible effects happen. The lights on the outside and inside of the cone should flash, the cone should raise up and then lower down close to the body and then raise up again. GORGO can do this with a block and tackle arrangement or it can be done off stage. A strobe light gives a good effect, colored lights above the ceiling and flash pots if available are most effective. The effects in this scene are up to the production staff but the more the better, and the greater the thunder and lightning are the more effective it all will be. ELIZABETH cowers against HENRY, HELLSTROM is fascinated)* It is over. *(He has pulled final switch up again)* Gorgo, we must remove the shield.

GORGO: Yes, Master.

*(They remove the shield and store it against the wall.)*

VICTOR: The electricity has been transferred to the body.

GORGO: My friend he lives?

HELLSTROM: *(Starts forward)* Did it work, Victor? Is there life?

VICTOR: *(Pushes him back)* Stand back. Let me see.

*(Goes above the body with his stethoscope.)*

ELIZABETH: *(Whispers)* Henry, I'm frightened.

HENRY: It's all right. I'm here.

HELLSTROM: Well? Speak, Victor Frankenstein, is it successful?

GORGO: My friend? My friend? Does he live?

VICTOR: *(As he listens)* I think I heard – I'm not sure but I think I heard a heartbeat. Was it only my imagination, my desire to hear it? *(Listens again)* No, there is nothing now, no life.

HELLSTROM: Victor, my boy, you could not expect –

VICTOR: *(On verge of hysteria, he crosses L)* Failed. I have failed. After so much hard work and so long a time ... so long –

HELLSTROM: It is for the best, I am sure.

VICTOR: Failed ... failed ... failed ... *(Stops and listens)* Wait. What was that?

HENRY: What?

HELLSTROM: I heard nothing.

VICTOR: Yes. Listen. *(After a moment there is a slight groan from under the sheet. He goes above the table)* There. You heard it, didn't you? Tell me you heard it.

HELLSTROM: A sound, yes.

VICTOR: It lives. My creation lives.

GORGO: My friend is alive.

ELIZABETH: Henry, it can't be.

HENRY: Is it possible?

VICTOR: *(The above speeches have overlapped as he goes to L of table)* It lives. It lives. It lives!

HENRY: *(There is a movement under the sheet)* Look it's moving.

HELLSTROM: Can it think?

HENRY: If so, what does it think?

*(The CREATURE moves to sitting position with his feet over down stage side of table but the sheet remains over him.)*

ELIZABETH: Is it human?

HENRY: What does it look like?

GORGO: My friend.

*(Starts for it but VICTOR holds him back.)*

VICTOR: No, Gorgo, stand back.

GORGO: But –

VICTOR: Back, I say.

*(The CREATURE stands below the table. He makes some guttural sounds and tries to bring his arms up but the sheet impedes him. He turns up stage.)*

GORGO: Let me help you, friend.

*(Goes above CREATURE and pulls the sheet off.)*

VICTOR: Leave him alone, you fool!
GORGO: *(Sees the CREATURE and recoils in horror)*
No, no, you are not human. No, you are ugly. Not my friend.
No, no –

*(Strikes out at him but the CREATURE hits him to the floor.
Dead silence as the CREATURE slowly turns front and
we get our first look at him. He is large and well-padded,
he wears a black wig which is thin and ragged. His
make-up is left to the imagination of the production, but
he should be very pale and towards the blue-green
shades. A combination of zinc oxide and gentian make
an effective base color. A layer of Latex over some
wrinkled tissue gives a good effect. His lips are gray and
his arms hang out from his black shirt and we see the
stitch marks from where the hands were sewn on. If the
hands are covered with liquid white shoe polish it gives
a good effect. There are other scars on his face which
rarely makes an expression. He expresses his feelings
mostly with his hands. He moves slowly and awkwardly
as he tries to acclimate himself to where and what he is.
ELIZABETH gives a stifled scream and turns into
HENRY, GORGO scampers away on his knees and the
others remain transfixed. A crescendo of music if it is
used and blackout.)*

## CURTAIN

## ACT II

*(The sets are the same except for the living room which is now ELIZABETH's upstairs sitting room. A regulation window is UC, in it, a door with lock is DL, there is a large armoire on the UR wall with a chest below it making the R wall. This is used for clothing and also to sit upon. L, there is a large tapestry covering a large section of the wall. A chaise lounge is left of center with the head upstage. The DL playing area is now set with a table and three straight chairs. There are two beer steins on the table. The laboratory is the same except a lantern and matches are set by the table.)*
*(At rise HENRY is pacing in the sitting room.)*


FREDERICA: *(Enters from L)* Henry. I'm glad you've come.

HENRY: How's Elizabeth? Is she resting comfortably?

FREDERICA: *(Glances off left)* Yes, she is in there in her bedroom with Dr. Hellstrom. He says there is no need for any more sedatives, that Elizabeth is a remarkably strong young woman but we knew that, didn't we?

HENRY: Yes, of course.

FREDERICA: *(Goes below HENRY to the chest and sits)* But I still don't know exactly what happened in Victor's laboratory. He's hardly said a word in the two days since you carried Elizabeth back here. He goes up to the laboratory, stays for a few hours, comes back and sits out there in the

45

garden staring into space. What was it, Henry?

HENRY: *(Goes to her)* I've told you. It is an experiment which turned out rather differently than Victor had hoped.

FREDERICA: When you brought Elizabeth back home here, those first few hours when she was out of her head she kept talking about it being alive. What did she mean by "it"?

HENRY: She was referring to – well – part of Victor's Experiment.

FREDERICA: But creature? She said, "Creature" over and over again.

HENRY: She meant the –

*(Stops and turns away.)*

FREDERICA: *(Rises)* What? Tell me, Henry.

HENRY: You must know by now that Victor was trying to accomplish unthought of miracles.

FREDERICA: Yes, I have realized that.

HENRY: With such tests one cannot always be certain of the outcome.

FREDERICA: The result was not what he expected?

HENRY: He proved his theory but in some ways the test was not successful.

FREDERICA: What ways, Henry? Tell me. I am Elizabeth's guardian. I am Victor's aunt. I am not a child. Tell me. I must know.

HENRY: *(Turns front)* Victor has succeeded in a scientific breakthrough always thought impossible.

FREDERICA: But with science these days nothing seems impossible short of creating –

*(Stops and stares at him.)*

HENRY: *(After a pause, he turns to her)* Yes.

FREDERICA: – life itself?

HENRY: He has accomplished that.

FREDERICA: Our Victor has actually created life, created a living cell?

HENRY: Not only a cell.

FREDERICA: Then what?

HENRY: Aunt Frederica, he has brought life to a complete body.

FREDERICA: A person already pronounced dead?

HENRY: No, a person he made from parts of many cadavers.

FREDERICA: *(Sits down on chest)* But that's impossible.

HENRY: So we thought. Even Dr. Hellstrom doubted it could be done.

FREDERICA: But this – this creature, where is it now?

HENRY: In the laboratory deeply sedated. We are only waiting for Victor to realize it must be destroyed.

FREDERICA: But you cannot destroy it, nor if it is alive.

HENRY: It is not alive, not as we know life. It is not a body with – what should I say? – a soul. It has the brain of a man who had no conscience. It is not a human, it is not an animal, it is just a creature.

BERTA: *(Comes bounding in from L)* Excuse me, Ma'am, but I best tell cook how many will be for dinner.

FREDERICA: The two of us and Dr. Hellstrom, I am sure, but I don't know about Victor. He is in the garden. You best ask him, Berta.

BERTA: Yes, Ma'am. Is he feeling all right? He looks right poorly.

FREDERICA: He's fine, Berta.

BERTA: *(Smiles to HENRY)* It must be the comparison to you, sir. You look so healthy.

HENRY: Thank you, Berta.

BERTA: I'll ask Mr. Victor about dinner. *(Goes to door and turns)* Oh, and Miss Elizabeth will be joining you.

FREDERICA: Oh, no, she must rest.

BERTA: No, Ma'am. I just helped her dress. She says she is feeling right proper.

FREDERICA: We're so glad to hear it.

BERTA: Queer turn she took, wasn't it, sir?

HENRY: Yes, indeed.

BERTA: She keeps talking about another person, a strange man. Should I tell cook this person might be joining you for dinner?

FREDERICA: No, Berta.

HENRY: *(With a glance to FREDERICA)* I hardly think so.

BERTA: Don't want anyone to suddenly pop in and surprise us, do we?

HENRY: Not this someone.

BERTA: Thank you, sir.

*(Exits)*

HENRY: I'm so glad and more than a little surprised that Elizabeth is up and about.

FREDERICA: *(Rises)* This creature you speak of, Henry, if it is dangerous then should it be left alone up there?

HENRY: Even after the sedation wears off it is well secured, believe me, and Victor's assistant is there to keep guard.

FREDERICA: I only saw this helper once and from a distance but I fear he is not as well versed in science as Victor is.

HENRY: I am sure not.

*(HELLSTROM comes in supporting a rather weak ELIZABETH.)*

HELLSTROM: Here you are, my dear.

ELIZABETH: Please, Dr. Hellstrom, I am not going to fall over. I feel quite strong.

FREDERICA: Are you sure you should get up?

ELIZABETH: Yes, Aunt.

HENRY: You had us very worried.

ELIZABETH: *(As she is helped to rest on the chaise. HENRY moves above the chaise and HELLSTROM sits on bottom edge of it)* I fear I was not prepared for the other evening.

FREDERICA: From what I hear no one would be.

VICTOR: *(Comes in the doorway)* And what do you hear? Who has been telling you things he shouldn't?

HENRY: I did, Victor. Aunt Frederica has a right to know what has happened.

FREDERICA: *(Rises)* And I want to know what *will* happen, Victor.

VICTOR: *(Crosses to window)* I'm not sure. I have crossed a threshold and I cannot turn back.

*(Lights dim up on laboratory and remain on the sitting room.
GORGO is looking out the door down the stairs, closes
the door and crosses to the window to look out.)*

HELLSTROM: You know what you must do, Victor. It
will be a kindness not only to us but to the creature as well.

HENRY: *(Goes to VICTOR)* It is the same as with a
wounded animal.

VICTOR: But is this thing wounded?

ELIZABETH: Victor, you cannot keep it chained up
there forever. Suppose it were to get out. Look at how it
behaved towards Gorgo and he was being kind.

HENRY: I feel sorry for Gorgo. He wanted a friend.

VICTOR: He wanted someone who was everything he is
not, a companion to show the world he is not alone and
abandoned.

HELLSTROM: But when he tore off the sheet he was
horrified.

VICTOR: His disappointment has turned to hatred.

HENRY: Is it safe to leave him alone with the creature?

VICTOR: Gorgo is my assistant. He has worked with me
from the beginning. No matter his feelings he will not destroy
our work.

HELLSTROM: Are you positive?

VICTOR: *(At window looking up towards the
laboratory)* I am sure all is calm.

*(Screech from the CREATURE off stage DR. GORGO goes to
the small opening in the downstage door and yells
through it.)*

GORGO: Quiet! Quiet! *(Another screech)* Stay down there. Stay in your chains or I shall whip you again. It's what you deserve. You are no friend. You are nothing.

*(Screech from the CREATURE.)*

ELIZABETH: *(Continuing on as they cannot hear the exchange in the laboratory)* Victor, what are you going to do?
VICTOR: Think. I must think.
GORGO: *(As the others exchange looks)* Stay there! Stay chained till the Master destroys you. I shall help him take you apart piece by piece.

*(Scream from the CREATURE and sound of chains being ripped out of the wall.)*

HENRY: *(To VICTOR quietly)* You know what must happen.
HELLSTROM: We can start over, a new beginning.
GORGO: *(Looks through the small opening in the door)* No! No! No! You broke the chains! You're a monster! Stay back!
FREDERICA: Victor, listen to the doctor, please.
GORGO: *(Terrified, he lights the lantern from table L)* Light. Light. He fears the light of flame.
VICTOR: Yes, I know what must be done, but not yet. Let me examine the creature further. Let me study him some more.
HENRY: Don't wait too long.
ELIZABETH: When I think of it I can still see that creature. Oh, Aunt Frederica, it was horrible. Horrible.

FREDERICA: But are you sure what's going on up there? Is it safe?

*(GORGO has taken lantern to the door and holds it up to torment the CREATURE.)*

VICTOR: I think so. I hope so.

*(Glances up that way.)*
*(The laboratory door bursts down, ripped from its hinges. This can be done with some lath holding the door in place since it is never opened any other time. GORGO holds the lantern to the CREATURE's face but he backs up in fright.)*

GORGO: Fire! Fire! Fire! You hate flame! Back! Back!
VICTOR: *(As a terrified GORGO retreats from the CREATURE)* I am not sure. Perhaps I should go back up there.
HELLSTROM: I'll come with you.

*(CREATURE knocks the lantern from GORGO's hand and grabs him by the neck. GORGO struggles for a moment and then goes limp. The CREATURE throws him aside as the lights fade on the laboratory. The CREATURE, in darkness, retreats to the bench R, under the panels, and sits.)*

HENRY: *(As we see VICTOR and HELLSTROM exit, he goes to ELIZABETH)* I'll stay with Elizabeth.
ELIZABETH: God be with you, Victor.

FREDERICA: *(Goes to her)* You should rest, Elizabeth.

ELIZABETH: I am better now knowing the creature will be destroyed, that no one else will have to look upon it. Yes, I am feeling much better.

FREDERICA: If you're sure?

ELIZABETH: It's so good to have you with us, Henry.

FREDERICA: *(With a smile)* Yes, so I have noticed.

ELIZABETH: Peace. Peace and quiet is with us again.

*(Lights dim and come up DL area where there is a table and 3 chairs. Two men are seated at the table with beer steins before them. Above the table is HORST and to the L is the SECOND MAN. They are both local workers and can be doubled from the GRAVE DIGGERS. The SECOND MAN is quite drunk.)*

HORST: *(As they toast)* To good health and prosperity.

SECOND: *(They drink)* Prosperity? I like that. I don't have no acquaintance with prosperity but I know I would enjoy it.

HORST: We're better off than some. We got two big landholders here. They take care of us and our families, don't they?

SECOND: *(Nodding his head)* That they do.

HORST: Good deal better than other villages. That I know for sure.

SECOND: For sure.

*(Drinks)*

HORST: I don't mind tellin' you I had my worries when old Baron Frankenstein died.

SECOND: Had my worries, too.

HORST: But that Miss Frederica, she took over right proper. A great lady, that one.

SECOND: *(Continues his nodding at all remarks)* Great. Yes, great.

HORST: She's carried on just the same as if the Baron was still with us.

SECOND: He's gone though.

HORST: I know that.

SECOND: You know that.

HORST: Between the Frankenstein and the Lovitz families we are damn lucky.

SECOND: Yes, damn.

HORST: But now that young Victor Frankenstein has returned I have me doubts.

SECOND: My doubts, too.

HORST: There's odd things goin' on.

SECOND: Most odd. Yes, odd. That's the word for it. Odd.

HORST: That abandoned mill young Victor turned into a workin' place, there's strange things goin' on up there.

SECOND: Strange. Other night durin' the storm there was bright lights up there as bright as the lightnin'. I thought maybe it was the beer makin' me see things but no, my old lady saw them, too. Bright lights.

HORST: And the Frankenstein Manor House there's odd things, too.

SECOND: Your girl been talkin' out of turn?

HORST: *(Getting angry)* My Berta's a good girl, she is.

SECOND: A good girl, yes, but what does this good girl say?

HORST: You'll hear for yourself. I told her, if she could get away, to meet me here.

SECOND: Then we'll hear from the horse's mouth.

HORST: *(Threatening him)* What's that?

SECOND: – as it were. Not that Berta's a horse. No, but we'll get information straight from the – from her mouth.

BERTA: *(Comes rushing in from R)* I only got a minute, Dad. I'm on an errand for Cook.

HORST: Sit down, m'dear.

SECOND: *(As BERTA sits in chair R)* Evenin', Berta.

BERTA: Hear you wife's feelin' poorly.

SECOND: She's always been poorly, always will be poorly.

HORST: Tell us what's doin' at the Manor.

BERTA: There's somethin' goin' on all right. I told you Miss Elizabeth took to her bed after they carried her in.

SECOND: From where?

BERTA: I think from Dr. Frankenstein's laboratory. They was chatterin' away about somethin' goin' on up there. Anyways, she's up and about again and that Dr. Hellstrom –

HORST: *(Explaining to SECOND MAN)* That's the doctor from Vienna what's supposed to have stayed one night but he's still here.

BERTA: He's stayin' with us at the Manor now. He's helpin' take care of Miss Elizabeth and he seems to know a lot about what's goin' on up at the mill. Him and that nice, handsome Mr. Henry, they're up there right now.

HORST: Why? For what?

BERTA: They was talkin' about whether to destroy somethin' or not.

SECOND: Destroy somethin'?

HORST: Yes, but what?

BERTA: I don't rightly know but whatever it is it sent Miss Elizabeth into a collapse and it's worryin' all of them.

*(Rises and looks towards laboratory.)*

HORST: What could they be goin' to destroy?

BERTA: What indeed?

*(Lights fade out and come up on the laboratory. The broken door has been removed during previous scene. The CREATURE is collapsed on the bench R. He is either dead or asleep as his head rests on his chest.)*

HELLSTROM: *(Off stage)* Yes, Gorgo is dead. His neck has been broken.

VICTOR: *(Off stage)* But where is the creature? The outside door was still locked.

HELLSTROM: *(Off stage)* He must be up there in the laboratory.

VICTOR: *(Off stage)* Come on.

HELLSTROM: *(Off stage)* Be careful. You've seen what he can do.

VICTOR: *(In a hushed whisper as they enter as he sees the CREATURE)* There.

HELLSTROM: *(Comes down below the table)* Is he still alive?

VICTOR: *(Goes to CREATURE)* Yes, he's alive.

HELLSTROM: How much better if he weren't.

VICTOR: *(Crosses to him)* But, Dr. Hellstrom, think of what we can learn from him, from this first creation of mankind. Does he think? Does he feel? Does he have emotions?

HELLSTROM: Does he have a soul?

VICTOR: *(Turns to CREATURE)* We must find out more.

HELLSTROM: He kills, that we know.

VICTOR: *(Crosses to CREATURE)* Poor Gorgo tormented him because he was not perfection. But we are scientists, Doctor, we can study and learn.

HELLSTROM: Is his heart rate as slow as before? Perhaps he is in a coma?

VICTOR: *(Puts his head down on CREATURE's chest listening to his heartbeat)* No, its heart is –

*(CREATURE jumps up with a loud cry. VICTOR steps back.)*

HELLSTROM: Look out!

VICTOR: *(Holds his hands out to the CREATURE)* Down, calm down. Calm down. It's all right. It's all right.

*(CREATURE holds his hands out wanting something.)*

HELLSTROM: He wants something.

VICTOR: Yes, but what?

HELLSTROM: *(As CREATURE puts his hands on VICTOR's face very friendly)* He knows who you are. He knows you created him.

VICTOR: *(To CREATURE)* Yes, yes, I am your friend. You can trust me.

HELLSTROM: He is looking to you for guidance.

VICTOR: *(Takes his hands down and speaks to him*

*slowly)* It's all right. We understand what you did. Gorgo tormented you. He was bad. *(At GORGO's name, the CREATURE puts his hands up in front of his face and gives an anguished cry. VICTOR takes his hands)* But what you did to him, it was wrong. That is something you will have to learn.

HELLSTROM: Is he not too young to be taught?

VICTOR: But he has an adult's brain.

HELLSTROM: *(Crosses to the table and picks up the tray of instruments, pencil and pads, a rubber ball, etc.)* Hands him something. See what he does with it.

VICTOR: *(Takes a pencil from the tray to DC and hands it to CREATURE)* Here, take this. *(CREATURE takes it and breaks it in half, throws it on the floor and puts hands out wanting more. VICTOR hands him a pad and puts the tray on the oper ~ting table. The CREATURE rips the pad and throws it down. VICTOR picks up the ball)* Here, take this ball. I used it for other tests.

*(He bounces it. CREATURE takes it and bounces it. He is delighted. Does it again and kneels on floor with the ball bouncing it.)*

HELLSTROM: He's like a child.

VICTOR: *(As CREATURE holds the ball lovingly to his cheek)* Somehow he seems contented, doesn't he?

HELLSTROM: Dare we leave him like this?

VICTOR: The bottom door is too strong even for him to break down. We must take Gorgo out and bury him.

HELLSTROM: But where?

VICTOR: Does it matter?

HELLSTROM: The cemetery?

VICTOR: It can't be.

HELLSTROM: But should he not be in consecrated ground?

VICTOR: No one must know what happened here. We are scientists, Doctor, we must let nothing stand in the way of our work.

HELLSTROM: Once again I find the student is right. Let us go.

VICTOR: Come, let us get it over with.

HELLSTROM: *(Looks at CREATURE playing with the ball. He suddenly hits it rather soundly)* I have a feeling – no, never mind. I am sure he will be all right.

*(He exits.)*

VICTOR: *(Pauses at the door)* He looks even a bit happy, doesn't he? *(Exits, closes door, and we hear him off stage)* I'll bolt the downstairs door.

*(CREATURE plays with the ball, it rolls away, he rises and gets another pencil from the tray. He breaks it and picks up the entire tray, takes the scalpel from it and it cuts his finger causing him to throw the tray down. He picks it up, suddenly pauses looking in it as he sees himself for the first time. He moves one hand across his face and sees it in the reflection. He stares in shock and throws the tray down and puts both hands over his face and then raises them straight up to heaven with a tremendous scream of pain. Blackout. In the dark he crosses UC with the tray and stands looking out the window.)*

*(Music, if used, fades and lights come up DL area. The table and chairs have been removed since this is in the village square. HORST and the SECOND MAN are conversing. There is a loud call from the back of the audience if used or from R. It is JALNA, she can be doubled if desired with the MOTHER from the first scene.)*

JALNA: *(Comes running down the aisle or on stage)* Horst! Horst!

HORST: Who's there? Who calls?

JALNA: Horst!

SECOND: It's Jalna.

JALNA: Horst, thank the lord you're here.

HORST: What's wrong?

JALNA: It's what I just seen.

SECOND: Where? Up where you live?

JALNA: Should I see the Burgomaster? My husband has taken a card full of produce into the city and I am all alone but I seen it. I know I seen it.

HORST: Calm down, Jalna, and tell me what you seen.

JALNA: It was dark it was. I was just standin' on the porch gettin' a breath of fresh air before goin' to bed. The moon was in and out of the clouds –

HORST: Yes, go on.

JALNA: Not like that storm t'other night. I never seen one like that in all my born days.

HORST: But just now? What did you see just now?

JALNA: I was standin' there and when the moon come out from behind a cloud, I saw two men crossin' the field up there.

HORST: What's so bad with that?

JALNA: They was carryin' somethin'.

SECOND: What?

JALNA: A man. They was carryin' a man.

HORST: *(With a laugh)* Most likely two buddies helpin' another who had a bit too much at the pub.

JALNA: No, this man was lifeless. His head hung down funny-like. He was dead. I could see that. I tell you he was dead.

HORST: Where was they takin' him?

JALNA: They went off into the woods, they did, and just as I started down here they come out again – alone. The body was gone.

SECOND: Does seem we ought to report it, don't you think so, Horst?

HORST: It's our duty.

JALNA: Hold! I am not positive but I am quite certain that one of them was that doctor who came into the village and –

SECOND: Yes.

JALNA: – Dr. Frankenstein.

HORST: But why him?

SECOND: What would those men be doin' with a body?

JALNA: *(To HORST)* I know your Berta has been sayin' some strange things is goin' on at the Manor.

SECOND: And at the old mill.

JALNA: What should I do? I don't want to cause no trouble for the Frankensteins, them bein' such good people and all.

HORST: *(Goes below BERTA to look up towards the laboratory)* If it was Dr. Frankenstein you seen then there was nothin' wrong. Strange things have been goin' on, it's a fact, but that man could not be doin' evil.

JALNA: But if it was him, then what is goin' on up there in that mill? What is Victor Frankenstein doing?

*(The three turn and look up towards the laboratory as music in, if it is used, and lights come up on the laboratory. The CREATURE is standing looking out the window with his back to the audience. He holds the silver tray in front of him but it is not visible to the audience. VICTOR enters followed by HELLSTROM who goes DL as VICTOR closes the door. They speak as they enter.)*

VICTOR: It was good of you to say a few words over Gorgo.

HELLSTROM: It seemed appropriate, the poor fellow.

VICTOR: *(Sees CREATURE, sotto voice)* Our patient seems calm now.

HELLSTROM: Look! *(Sees instruments on the floor)* What's he been up to?

VICTOR: *(Crosses down)* My instruments. They're ruined.

*(Picks up instruments and hands them to HELLSTROM who puts them on table L.)*

HELLSTROM: You can see this creature has no control over what he does. He does not think as we do. He has no basis for right and wrong. He must be destroyed.

VICTOR: *(Crosses to DR his eyes constantly on the CREATURE)* A set-back. Perhaps this is only a set-back. Let me try to make him understand. Let me speak to him.

*(He slowly starts to walk towards the CREATURE.)*

HELLSTROM: Take care!

*(The CREATURE slowly turns. VICTOR stops. The CREATURE slowly and without taking his eyes off VICTOR moves towards him step by step. When he is almost to him he suddenly holds up the tray to VICTOR's face and then to his own.)*

VICTOR: He sees himself, his own reflection.
HELLSTROM: Come back, Victor.

*(CREATURE hurls the tray onto the floor and backs VICTOR up slowly toward DC.)*

VICTOR: *(His eyes never leaving the CREATURE he speaks softly to HELLSTROM)* The hypodermic. It was there on the table. Where is it now, on the floor?

HELLSTROM: *(Finds it)* Yes, it is here and it is still full.

VICTOR: *(As the CREATURE continues to advance on him)* Get behind him quickly.

HELLSTROM: *(As he creeps up)* Don't do anything sudden. Keep very calm.

VICTOR: *(To CREATURE)* There, there. *(Holds out his hands in friendship)* It's all right. You'll be all right. *(CREATURE suddenly lunges at him and grabs him by the throat)* Doctor, quick!

*(HELLSTROM stabs the needle into the CREATURE's back making the CREATURE let go of VICTOR and stagger backwards against the table.)*

HELLSTROM: It's working!

*(The CREATURE backs down sitting on the table and he gives an odd cry of bewilderment and his hands pass in front of his blurring eyes as he faints.)*

VICTOR: Grab him, Doctor!
HELLSTROM: Help him onto the table.

*(They help CREATURE to lie down on the table with his head to the R.)*

VICTOR: He was so strong.
HELLSTROM: How long will this shot last?
VICTOR: It would kill an ordinary man but him, I don't know. Hours anyway, perhaps all night.
HELLSTROM: What do you have that's lethal? We must destroy him and bury him like we did Gorgo, leave no trace of what has happened here. No one must know ever.
VICTOR: *(Gets vial from table L, fills hypodermic with it and hands it to HELLSTROM)* Here, Doctor, surely this is more than a fatal dose.
HELLSTROM: Do you want to do it or shall I?
VICTOR: *(Holds him back)* Not yet, please. Cannot we wait a few days and –
HELLSTROM: No, Victor, you said that before and you've been proved wrong. You were almost killed a few minutes ago. This beast must be done away with.
VICTOR: But I created him. I can't destroy him. I can't.
HELLSTROM: *(Pushes him L towards the door)* Let me do it. You go back to Elizabeth, to the life you knew before

all this. Go, I will take care of everything and we will never mention this again to a soul.

VICTOR: But I can't.

HELLSTROM: Go! *(VICTOR goes to door, turns for one final look and goes. HELLSTROM checks the hypodermic, examines the CREATURE from below the operating table. If music is used it can start now. As he leans down to listen to the CREATURE's heart we see the CREATURE's hand starts to move and it raises high above HELLSTROM and blackout. In the dark we hear HELLSTROM's final cry)* No, no! God help me! No!

*(Lights come up on ELIZABETH's sitting room. She is lying on the chaise and VICTOR is pacing.)*

ELIZABETH: Victor, sit down and rest yourself, please. You're only going to make yourself ill.

VICTOR: *(Goes to window)* Dr. Hellstrom should have returned by now.

ELIZABETH: You said you were certain he would do some tests. He's a scientist and who knows better than you how they do carry on.

VICTOR: *(Turns to her with a smile)* You are a marvelous person, Elizabeth.

ELIZABETH: Oh tosh!

VICTOR: You are and you deserve a better life than I can give you.

ELIZABETH: Nonsense. *(Sits up)* We shall have the best marriage in the history of mankind. We've always known that right from the beginning.

VICTOR: That's what worries me.

ELIZABETH: What?

VICTOR: That we've always known. Always. We've grown, we've changed. I still love you more than you know but I am so tied to my work that I wonder if it is not the most important thing to me.

ELIZABETH: I would rather share you with a laboratory than with another woman.

VICTOR: *(Moves away R)* This experiment, this creature I have created, look what it has done to me. I cannot sleep from worrying whether I have brought about good or evil, right or wrong. It is there in my mind all the time till I think I – *(Goes to the window almost breaking down)* Forgive me. I should not let you see me like this.

ELIZABETH: *(Goes to him)* It will be all right now that this creature is gone. It will be like it was before.

VICTOR: Before? *(Moves DR)* Can we ever go back? Can we ever be the same again? You saw what I did. It revolted you but I know I cannot stop. I will go on and on further into the unknown until – I cannot ask you to share such a life, can I?

ELIZABETH: *(Crosses to him)* I have known for a long time now that I am but a part of your life and I accept that.

VICTOR: I fear I am incapable of offering you more.

ELIZABETH: I know.

VICTOR: We three grew up together, you and me and Henry. It was so natural for us to become engaged. Everyone expected it. We do have love for each other, I know that, but there is Henry and I –

ELIZABETH: No, Victor, stop right there.

VICTOR: Am I being selfish in keeping you from a fuller life with him?

ELIZABETH: No, no, please.

VICTOR: I am certain you have feelings for him and I know he loves you.

ELIZABETH: Never has a word passed between us that would indicate that we have more than a deep affection.

HENRY: *(Has entered during the above)* Never, Victor, I assure you.

ELIZABETH: Henry!

VICTOR: *(Goes to him)* I'm glad you heard. I have been trying to find the right time to step aside if it is what you both want.

HENRY: You must believe I have never approached Elizabeth in any way.

VICTOR: But I have seen the way you look at her, the way you talk to her. I know, Henry, my friend.

HENRY: What I know is that I am to be the best man at your wedding and I shall be so happy for both of you on that day.

ELIZABETH: Thank you, Henry.

VICTOR: I have always known what a true friend you were but never more than at this moment.

HENRY: Then let us speak no more about it. Come, why do we not go out into the garden and get some color back in Elizabeth's cheeks?

ELIZABETH: No. Victor is too worried about Dr. Hellstrom.

HENRY: Would it make you feel better if we went up to the laboratory to make sure he's all right?

VICTOR: Yes, yes it would.

ELIZABETH: Go along you two and bring back some good news.

HENRY: *(Goes to door with VICTOR)* We'll hurry.

VICTOR: You rest, Elizabeth.

ELIZABETH: *(Stops them at the door)* Wait. A word with both of you. *(They turn)* I love you both very much. I want to be sure you know that.

VICTOR: We do.

*(They leave. ELIZABETH goes to the window and looks out towards the laboratory.)*

BERTA: *(Enters)* Miss.

ELIZABETH: Yes, Berta.

BERTA: It looks like the gentlemen is goin' out again. Does that mean no tea?

ELIZABETH: I'm afraid so, Berta, just one cup for me.

BERTA: Cook will be that upset, she will. She baked them nice little cakes you all like so much.

ELIZABETH: Just bring me a cup, Berta, and why don't you have a cake or two? We won't tell cook.

BERTA: *(With a huge smile)* Oh, thank you, Miss.

*(Exits)*

ELIZABETH: *(Looking out)* Take care, both of you. God be with you.

*(Lights dim and come up on the laboratory. HELLSTROM is lying face up on the operating table, his head L.)*

VICTOR: *(Off stage calling)* Dr. Hellstrom. Dr. Hellstrom.

HENRY: *(Off stage)* Look, Victor. The door.

VICTOR: *(Off stage)* That's impossible.

HENRY: *(Off stage)* It's ripped from its hinges.

VICTOR: *(Off stage)* Quick, Henry, up here!

HENRY: *(Sound of footsteps as they approach. Off stage)* The creature? Watch out!

VICTOR: *(Rushes in followed by HENRY)* Dr. Hellstrom!

HENRY: There! The table!

VICTOR: *(They see him stretched across the table. Goes to him)* Doctor –

HENRY: *(Joins him above table)* Good God!

VICTOR: *(Lifts HELLSTROM's head)* Broken. His neck has been crushed.

HENRY: The creature. Where is it?

VICTOR: *(Goes to window and looks out)* He could be anywhere by now.

HENRY: What can he be doing out there?

VICTOR: Don't you see, he's looking for me.

HENRY: Why only you?

VICTOR: *(Goes down below table)* He blames me for his very existence. That's why he attacked me before once he realized what he was.

HENRY: *(Joins him below table)* He killed Gorgo and now Dr. Hellstrom. He may be after everyone who was here when he was given life. That means you and me and – good God, Elizabeth.

VICTOR: Do you realize what this means?

HENRY: What?

VICTOR: He thinks, he has emotions. He feels.

HENRY: Yes, he feels revenge.

VICTOR: That's what he is seeking now.

*(Goes to window.)*

HENRY: But he wouldn't harm anyone he didn't know, would he?

VICTOR: No, I think he's just after us unless –

HENRY: Unless what?

VICTOR: *(Crosses down)* Unless someone angers him.

HENRY: Then who knows what he might do.

VICTOR: *(Looks out over audience)* He is out there somewhere alone, by himself, a creature with no conscience. What is he doing? Where is he?

*(Lights dim as we hear a young girl singing DL. Lights come up on MARIA who is playing Jacks. She is a peasant girl of seven or eight years and is dressed in clean old clothes. She bounces the ball, picks up the jacks, and continues. After a moment there is a sound of footsteps. If the theatre aisle is used the CREATURE can come down that and be making small guttural noises. If he comes on stage it should be from R.)*

MARIA: *(She rises)* Come and play with me. I hear you. Where are you? Come here. I don't want to play hide and seek. *(Footsteps grow closer)* Come out, come out, wherever you are. *(The CREATURE appears before her. They look at each other for a moment, MARIA is scared for a moment but then overcomes it)* Who are you? You look so sad. Are you ill? You need someone to play with, don't you? Do you know how to play Jacks? Come on, I'll show you. *(She takes the*

*CREATURE's hand. He steps closer to her. He puts his hand on her face admiring it)* Now these are jacks and this is the ball. *(Holds the ball out and immediately the CREATURE is excited and reaches for it)* Now, you bounce the ball like this and then pick up as many jacks as you can. Now, it's your turn. *(Hands him the ball and she puts the jacks on the ground CREATURE bounces the ball but is not very successful with the jacks)* Now it is my turn. *(MARIA goes to take the ball back. CREATURE holds it to him and grunts)* Come on, it's my turn. Give me the ball. *(She goes to take it from him, but he refuses to let it go squealing all the time)* Give me the ball! It's mine! Give it to me!

*(She gets it away from him. She backs away as he approaches her to get the ball. As he reaches out to grab her, blackout and we hear her scream. Lights come up on the sitting room. ELIZABETH is holding a dress which she is folding by the bench.)*
*(This scene must be played with great urgency. ELIZABETH is packing and clothes are on the chest and chaise. VICTOR enters carrying a suitcase which he puts on the chaise.)*

VICTOR: Just pack this one. There's no time to lose.

ELIZABETH: *(Puts dress down)* I don't want to leave, Victor. I'm sure it's quite unnecessary.

VICTOR: *(Goes to her)* You must go. Henry and I agree it is for your safety.

ELIZABETH: But this creature killed Dr. Hellstrom because he was about to harm him. I am in no danger.

VICTOR: He is around here somewhere so it is best you leave.

BERTA: *(Enters carrying a pressed dress)* Miss Elizabeth.

ELIZABETH: Yes, Berta.

BERTA: Here is your gown I pressed. May I help you with anything else? I'm a very good packer.

ELIZABETH: *(Takes dress from her and puts it on chaise)* Thank you, Berta, I shall call when I am ready.

BERTA: Will Mr. Henry be leaving, too?

VICTOR: No, he is staying with me.

BERTA: *(Huge smile)* I am so glad. Call when you want me, Miss.

ELIZABETH: I shall. *(BERTA exits)* Victor, come with me, I beg of you.

VICTOR: No. My place is here.

ELIZABETH: If it is not safe for me then it is much more dangerous for you.

VICTOR: I started this and I must finish it.

FREDERICA: *(Enters hurriedly)* I have telephoned my sister in Vienna. She is expecting us by early tomorrow morning.

ELIZABETH: There's no need for you to go, too, Aunt Frederica.

FREDERICA: I would not dream of letting you journey alone.

VICTOR: Besides, I insisted she accompany you.

ELIZABETH: Very well. Now I must pack. What to take. What to take?

*(She looks about the room as the lights fade and come up DL inset which is Village Square so has no set. JALNA and HORST are talking with the SECOND MAN.)*

HORST: ... and there is a body buried in the woods if that is what Jalna saw.

SECOND: And the noises we've heard from that laboratory of his. What are they?

JALNA: And in the woods I've heard strange sounds myself, odd sounds like moans and screams, nothing of this earth, I know that.

HORST: I tell you there is some kind of an animal Frankenstein's been doin' his experiments on, some kind of wild creature.

JALNA: And it's escaped.

SECOND: An escaped beast in our woods? That's it, I'm sure of it.

JALNA: *(Points down the aisle if it is used, otherwise points OR)* Who's that comin'?

HORST: It's Korda.

SECOND: What's he carryin'?

JALNA: Saints preserve us, it's Maria. It's his daughter.

HORST: My God.

KORDA: *(As he comes into the center of the group. He is carrying MARIA who is stretched out across his arms)* She is dead. My Maria is dead.

SECOND: How? What happened, Korda?

KORDA: Some monster, some animal, I don't know. I heard screams. I came running and Maria way lyin' there, her neck broke.

JALNA: Who could have done such a thing?

KORDA: I heard noises in the woods. I saw it stumbling away.

HORST: What was it?

KORDA: I don't know. It was too far away. It was just ... something ... some thing ...

*(Lights dim to black and come up on the dressing room.*
*ELIZABETH is by the suitcase on the chaise. VICTOR is*
*by the window and FREDERICA is crossing to*
*ELIZABETH.)*

FREDERICA: Let me help you Elizabeth. You must
hurry, it will be dark before we know it.

ELIZABETH: I still don't know why I should leave?
Why must I?

VICTOR: *(He has been pacing and now he turns from*
*the window speaking loud and strong)* Go! You must go, do
you hear!

ELIZABETH: *(Surprised at his outburst)* If you say so,
Victor.

HENRY: *(Bursts in from hallway)* Quickly! Come
quickly, Victor!

VICTOR: *(Goes to him)* What is it?

HENRY: Maria, Korda's daughter. She is dead.

ELIZABETH: Oh, no.

FREDERICA: *(At the same time)* The poor child.

VICTOR: Where did it happen?

HENRY: By the pond near her home.

ELIZABETH: Did she drown?

HENRY: She was murdered, her body broken.

VICTOR: The creature.

HENRY: The villagers are gathering in the Square. You
must talk to them before they start a search party without
knowing what or who they are after.

VICTOR: We must go. *(Goes below HENRY to the door*
*and turns back)* Aunt Frederica, stay here with Elizabeth. Do
not leave her alone for an instant.

ELIZABETH: *(Comes down)* Don't bother about me. Help the villagers.

VICTOR: This creature is around somewhere. He wants revenge. Stay with Elizabeth, Aunt Frederica, please.

FREDERICA: I shall.

VICTOR: Come, Henry.

*(They exit.)*

FREDERICA: *(Moves away R)* Little Maria. I cannot believe it. What is happening in our village?

ELIZABETH: Her poor mother. How can she face it?

FREDERICA: Her only child.

ELIZABETH: *(Goes to her)* You must go to her.

FREDERICA: Yes, I must help her if I can. *(Goes below ELIZABETH to door and stops)* No. I promised Victor I would stay with you.

ELIZABETH: Don't be silly. I'll be safe. I'll even lock the door.

FREDERICA: *(As she is pushed out)* You're quite sure?

ELIZABETH: I am positive. *(FREDERICA is out)* I am locking the door. *(She does so)* There, Aunt, the door is locked.

FREDERICA: *(Off stage)* Don't unlock it for anyone but us.

*(ELIZABETH is left alone. She opens the suitcase and packs an article away. Goes to the wardrobe and starts to open it and pauses.)*

ELIZABETH: Oh, no! Where did I put that scarf? Oh, yes.

*(Gets it from under dress on chaise and packs it. She heads
for the wardrobe again and is almost there when there is
a knock at the door.)*

BERTA: *(Off stage)* Miss Elizabeth.
ELIZABETH: Yes, Berta.
BERTA: *(Off stage)* You're sure I can't help?
ELIZABETH: No, I'm doing very well, thank you.
BERTA: *(Off stage)* All right, Miss. *(ELIZABETH heads
for the wardrobe again, pauses in front of it, opens it and
removes a piece of clothing. As she turns back towards the
chaise, the entire tapestry from the wall L comes ripping
down and the CREATURE stands behind it. She screams. He
leaps down and goes toward her as she faints C. He stands
over her and looks down. He puts his hands on her face and
then on his own disfigured one. He backs away with his hands
in front of his face as there is knocking on the door) (Off
stage)* Miss Elizabeth! Miss Elizabeth!

FREDERICA: *(At same time)* Elizabeth, what is it? Open
the door! Elizabeth!

*(The CREATURE escapes through the passageway behind
the panel as music comes up if used and lights fade to DL
area which is again the Village Square. HORST is
standing L with JALNA to his L and then KORDA and
SECOND MAN. It is assumed the audience is the crowds
in the Square.)*

HORST: *(As VICTOR and HENRY enter)* Dr.
Frankenstein, come, we need your help. We are going into the
woods, we are searching everywhere. There is a beast –

VICTOR: Listen to me first, I beg of you.

SECOND: Is this not your fault?

KORDA: Has this not come from your laboratory?

JALNA: The mill. We have heard.

KORDA: I have seen.

VICTOR: *(Talks out front)* Listen to me, all of you. I want you to know I am solely responsible for what has happened. I have taken science where no man should trespass and I, alone, will settle this. No one shall ever repeat my mistake.

*(He starts off.)*

HENRY: *(Goes to him and stops him)* Do you know where he is?

VICTOR: He was created in the laboratory and he must be returning there.

HENRY: To the scene of his birth, of course.

VICTOR: I am sure of it.

HENRY: I'll come with you.

VICTOR: No. I started this alone and I must finish it alone. I am well armed. *(Takes out pistol)* I will end my experiment. You take care of Elizabeth – always.

*(Rushes out and lights fade and come up on the laboratory. The CREATURE comes crashing through the door. He is more furious and deadly than we have seen him before. He comes down to R of the operating table and smashes the silver tray which is there onto the floor. We hear VICTOR's footsteps from outside. The CREATURE turns and stares at the door as VICTOR enters. VICTOR steps*

*down a step or two and they look at each other for a long
pause. VICTOR comes down a few more steps and the
CREATURE goes up to counter him)*

VICTOR: You knew I would come, didn't you? That's
why you came back here. You can think. You can reason.
*(Moves above table as CREATURE backs away down stage)*
Then you must know the end in inevitable. You have done
evil so I have done evil. We are both guilty. We are both
failures. *(CREATURE starts for him but he pulls out the
pistol. CREATURE doesn't know what it is but he is fearful of
it)* I only pray no one else will ever do what I have done.

*(CREATURE starts for him again but he shoots several times.
The CREATURE recoils and comes against the table
where he turns and beats the table in rage. He turns and
stumbles towards VICTOR in a final leap and grabs him
by the neck strangling him till VICTOR falls to the floor.
CREATURE crosses to door but he is unable to go
further, he turns and looks at the table where he was
born and manages to crawl up and is quiet. Lights stay
on him as they come up DL where FREDERICA is
standing L with HENRY to her R and ELIZABETH to his
R. They are in coats and hats. They look out front below
them where we assume VICTOR's coffin is.)*

ELIZABETH: Ashes to ashes, dust to dust.

*(Drops handful of dirt.)*

HENRY: Farewell, Victor, my good friend.

FREDERICA: We must forgive what he did.

HENRY: How many failures are there before one success? I must return to the laboratory and destroy what remains of Victor's work.

ELIZABETH: Should we not give the Creature a decent burial? Perhaps here in consecrated ground? Maybe he was human. The line is thin indeed.

HENRY: If you wish.

FREDERICA: Good and evil. What a struggle they had up there.

*(They all turn towards the laboratory.)*

HENRY: And the evil is gone.

ELIZABETH: Is it, Henry, or does what we do go on after we are gone?

HENRY: But he destroyed the evil. It is gone forever.

ELIZABETH: I wonder ... I wonder.

*(Lights dim to half on DL. Music starts if it is used. The CREATURE's hand slowly moves and comes out towards the audience as he almost sits up and the hand reaches straight out. Blackout.)*

## CURTAIN

## PROPERTIES

### ACT I:

**Scene 1:** Cemetery: coffin, bag with scalpel or large knife and a large cloth (GORGO), Kerchief (GORGO), Money (VICTOR), Shovel (GRAVE DIGGER)

**Scene 2:** Living room: tea tray with 2 cups, saucers, milk, spoons, plate of small sandwiches (BERTA)

**Scene 3:** Laboratory: on-stage – instruments, Brain in glass container, covered, Rubber gloves (VICTOR), Wrapped hand (GORGO)

**Scene 4:** Living room: knitting (ELIZABETH), Calling card (BERTA), Handkerchief in knitting basket (ELIZABETH)

**Scene 5:** Laboratory: Rubber gloves (VICTOR), Brain from previous scene, Instruments from previous scene

**Scene 6:** Hotel DL – 3 tea cups on table, Potted plant for decor, Smelling salts in Elizabeth's reticule, Table and three straight chairs

**Scene 7:** Laboratory: all equipment

### ACT II:

**Scene 1:** Elizabeth's sitting room and Laboratory: Lantern and matches in laboratory

**Scene 2:** DL Pub: table, 3 chairs, 2 steins of beer

**Scene 3:** Laboratory: pencils, pad on desk, ball on desk

**Scene 4:** DL Street Square: no props

**Scene 5:** Laboratory: syringe on floor, poison vial on desk or in cabinet

**Scene 6:** Elizabeth's room: no props

**Scene 7:** Laboratory: no props

**Scene 8:** DL Edge of woods: Ball and jacks

**Scene 9:** Elizabeth's room: Suitcase (HENRY)

## PROPERTY LIST

### ACT I:

**Preset:** On table L in laboratory, silver tray with instruments, covered jar with brain.

Tray with 3 teacups, saucer, spoons, sugar and creamer on table in DL inset.

**Off Right:** Doctors bag with cloth and knife or scalpel (GORGO).

Kerchief (GORGO).

Money (VICTOR).

Dummy body under sheet if used.

Fake hand wrapped in cloth (GORGO).

Stethoscope and rubber gloves (VICTOR).

**Off Left:** Shovel (FIRST GRAVE DIGGER).

Reticule with smelling salts (ELIZABETH).

Tea tray with 2 cups, spoons, sugar, creamer, and small plate of sandwiches (BERTA).

Embroidery and basket (ELIZABETH).

Calling card (BERTA).

Handkerchief (ELIZABETH).

### ACT II:

**Preset:** Lantern and matches by table L in laboratory.

Pencils, pad, rubber ball, hypodermic needle, vial of medicine on table L in laboratory.

3 beer steins table in DL inset.

**Off Right:** Suitcase (VICTOR).

Dress (BERTA).

Clothes including scarf preset on stage before packing scene.

Pistol (VICTOR).

Jacks and ball (MARIA).

Small handful of dirt (ELIZABETH).

# Other Publications for Your Interest

## LLOYD'S PRAYER
### (LITTLE THEATRE—COMEDY)
### By KEVIN KLING

3 men, 1 woman (1 man & 1 woman play various parts). Bare stage w/set pieces.

Be amazed! The author of the amazing *21A* has fashioned a hilarious comic parable about Bob, the Raccoon Boy, and what happens to him when he is "rescued" from the raccoons who raised him and taught what it means to be human. At first, Bob can only make whirring raccoon sounds, but he is taught to speak by a delightfully whacko "Mom and Dad". He is taken from his cage at Mom and Dad's house by an ambitious ex-con named Lloyd, who sees the raccoon boy as his ticket to fame and fortune. When his first idea— displaying Bob as a carny sideshow freak—fails, Lloyd gets the brilliant idea to become a religious evangelist, displaying Bob as another sort of freak: a miracle from God. Lloyd's pitch, a promise of inspiration "that will bring grown men to a sitting position and women to a greater understanding of themselves", makes them both celebrities. By this time, Bob speaks pretty well ("I've been called many things in my life...But I prefer 'Bob'"), and is on the verge of innocence corrupted when there appears on the scene a beautiful guardian angel, dressed as a high school cheerleader. "Be amazed!", she declares, admonishing Bob to beware of Lloyd. What ensues is an amusing tug-of-war between the angel and Lloyd, with Bob the Raccoon Boy as the rope. The unqualified hit of the Actors Theatre of Louisville 1988 Humana Festival, this brilliant new comedy is "a whirlwind of original humor that comes in waves."—Lexington Herald-Leader. "Fresh, funny and charming."— Columbus Dispatch. "Kling is quite simply a comic genius."—Dramatics Magazine.

(#13997)

## 21A
### (ADVANCED GROUPS—COMEDY)
### By KEVIN KLING

1 man—Bare stage w/chairs.

"Astonishing", was the way Newsweek Magazine summed up this one-man tour-de-force in which Mr. Kling performed all the riders on a Minneapolis city bus: eight characters, including the driver. Structured as a series of monologues which in "real life" are going on simultaneously, this hilarious and decidedly "different" play had them rolling in the aisles at Louisville's famed Humana Festival where it won the prestigious Heideman Award. Kling started with the droll driver and moved on to such odd-balls as Gladys, Chairman Francis (a religious proselytizer), Captain Twelve-Pack (a drunk with a beer 12-pack box over his head) and a businessman who is decidedly *not* "Dave", no matter how fervently Captain Twelve-Pack insists that he *is*. And: who is the mysterious intruder sitting at the back of the bus? "Stunning."—U.S.A. Today.

(#22237)

# Other Publications for Your Interest

## *EMERALD CITY*
### (LITTLE THEATRE—COMEDY)

### By DAVID WILLIAMSON
(author of the screenplays to "The Year of Living Dangerously" and Gallipoli")

#### 3 men, 3 women—Unit set

In "the trade"—i.e., the movie biz as covered by *Variety*—"Oz" is not over the rainbow but Down Under. Australia. Which makes Sydney the Emerald City, where there is not one wizard but a host of them, who are the Deal-Makers. Colin, a critically-praised but commercially under-successful screenwriter, and his wife Kate, an Editor, feel a change of venue is called for, from Melbourne (i.e., The Sticks) to Sydney, the Emerald City, the major leagues. There, Colin joins forces with an aggressive, fast-talking aspiring screen-writer named Mike, who has no discernible talent for writing but who is a genius at the Art of the Deal. Mike parlays his tenuous connection with Colin into a series of cinematic projects which culminate in his becoming a global tycoon, a pinnacle from which he can put many different projects into "development", such as Kate's pet project, a serious ab-original novel, which Mike plans to transplant to Tennessee as a vehicle for Eddie Murphy. Eventually, Colin and Kate must make a moral decision: is the Emerald City a sane place to be: or do they want to go back to Kansas? "Hype and Hypocrisy amusingly help to speed the plow on the road to *Emerald City*."—N.Y. Times. "Winsomely cynical."—Time Mag. "Funny and engaging...its characters must be as much fun to play as they are to listen to." —N.Y. Post. "An incisive, grimly graceful, painfully funny play...this examination of how the noble ambition for fame deteriorates into lust for money and power, and how relation-ships of every kind subsist on deception, deserves our delightedly undivided attention. *Emerald City* portrays human rivalry with maximum comic and dramatic effect because it is as humorous as it is witty."—N.Y. Mag.

(#7078)

## *THE FILM SOCIETY*
### (LITTLE THEATRE—DRAMATIC COMEDY

### By JON ROBIN BAITZ

#### 4 men, 2 women—Various interiors. (may be unit set).

Imagine the best of Simon Gray crossed with the best of Athol Fugard. The New York critics lavished praise upon this wonderful play, calling Mr. Baitz a major new voice in our theatre. *The Film Society*, set in South Africa, is *not* about the effects of apartheid—at least, overtly. Blenheim is a provincial private school modeled on the second-rate British education machine. It is 1970, a time of complacency for everyone but Terry, a former teacher at Blenheim, who has lost his job because of his connections with Blacks (he invited a Black priest to speak at Commencement). Terry tries to involve Jonathan, another teacher at the school and the central character in this play; but Jonathan cares only about his film society, which he wants to keep going at all costs—even if it means programming only safe, non-objectionable, films. When Jonathan's mother, a local rich lady, promises to donate a substantial amount of money to Blenheim if Jonathan is made Headmaster, he must finally choose which side he is on: Terry's or The Establishment's. "Using the school of a microcosm for South Africa, Baitz explores the psychological workings of repression in a society that has to kill its conscience in order to persist in a course of action it knows enough to abhor but cannot afford to relinquish."—New Yorker. "What distinguishes Mr. Baitz' writing, aside from its manifest literacy, is its ability to em-brace the ambiguities of political and moral dilemmas that might easily be reduced to blacks and whites."—N.Y. Times. "A beautiful, accomplished play...things I thought I was a churl still to value or expect—things like character, plot and theatre dialogue—really do matter."—N.Y. Daily News.

(#8123)

# Other Publications for Your Interest

## *MAGIC TIME*
### (LITTLE THEATRE—COMEDY)

### By JAMES SHERMAN

#### 5 men, 3 women—Interior

Off Broadway audiences and the critics enjoyed and praised this engaging backstage comedy about a troupe of professional actors (non-Equity) preparing to give their last performance of the summer in *Hamlet*. Very cleverly the backstage relationships mirror the onstage ones. For instance, Larry Mandell (Laertes) very much resents the performance of David Singer (Hamlet), as he feels *he* should have had the role. Also, he is secretly in love with Laurie Black (Ophelia)—who is living with David. David, meanwhile, is holding a mirror up to nature, but not to himself—and Laurie is trying to get him to be honest with her about his feelings. There's also a Horatio who has a thriving career in TV commercials; a Polonius who gave up acting to have a family and teach high school, but who has decidedly second thoughts, and a Gertrude and Claudius who are married in *real* life. This engaging play is an absolute *must* for all non-Equity groups, such as colleges, community theatres, and non-Equity pros or semi-pros. "There is an artful innocence in 'Magic Time' . . . It is also delightful."—N.Y. Times. ". . . captivating little backstage comedy . . . it is entirely winning . . . boasts one of the most entertaining band of Shakespearean players I've run across."—N.Y. Daily News. (#15028)

## *BADGERS*
### (LITTLE THEATRE—COMEDY)

### By DONALD WOLLNER

#### 6 men, 2 women—Interior, w/insert

"'Badgers! . . . opened the season at the Manhattan Punchline while Simon and Garfunkel were offering a concert in Central Park. In tandem, the two events were a kind of déjà vu for the 60's, when all things seemed possible, even revolution. As we watch 'Badgers' we can hear a subliminal 'Sounds of Silence'."—N.Y. Times. The time is 1967. The place is the University of Wisconsin during the Dow Chemical sit-in/riots. This cross-section of college campus life in that turbulent decade focuses on the effect of the events on the characters: "Wollner's amiable remembrance adds up to a sort of campus roll-call—here are radicalized kids from Eastern high schools, 'WASP' accountancy majors who didn't make Harvard or Penn. Most significant is the playwright's contention that none were touched lightly by those times . . . he has a strong sense of the canvas he's drawing on."—Soho Weekly News. If you loved *Moonchildren*, you're certain to love this "wry and gentle look at a toubled time" (Bergen Record). (#3998)

# Other Publications for Your Interest

## *GROWN UPS*
### (LITTLE THEATRE—COMEDY)
### By JULES FEIFFER

**2 men, 3 women, 1 female child—Interiors**

An acerbic comedy by the famed cartoonist and author of *Knock Knock* and *Little Murders*. It's about a middle-aged journalist who has, at last, grown-up—only to find he's trapped in a world of emotional infants. "A laceratingly funny play about the strangest of human syndromes—the love that kills rather than comforts. Feiffer's vision seems merciless, but its mercy is the fierce comic clarity with which he exposes every conceivable permutation of smooth-tongued cruelty . . . Feiffer constructs a fiendishly complex machine of reciprocal irritation in which Jake (the journalist), his parents, his wife and his sister carp, cavil, harass, hector and finally attack one another with relentless trivia that detonate deeply buried resentments like emotional land mines . . . Moving past Broadway one-liners and easy gags, (Feiffer) makes laughter an adventure . . . This farce is Feiffer's exclusive specialty, and it's never been more harrowingly hilarious."—Newsweek. "Savagely funny."—N.Y. Times. "A compelling, devastating evening of theatre . . . the first adult play of the season."—Women's Wear Daily. (#9125)

## *LUNCH HOUR*
### (LITTLE THEATRE—COMEDY)
### By JEAN KERR

**3 men, 2 women—Interior**

Never has Jean Kerr's wit had a keener edge or her comic sense more peaks of merriment than in this clever confection, starring Gilda Radner and Sam Waterston as a pair whose spouses are having an affair, and who have to counter by inventing an affair of their own. He, ironically, is a marriage counsellor, and a bit of a stick. His wife juggles husband, lover and mother and is a real go-getter. In fact, it was she who proposed to him. Of the other couple, the wife is a bit kooky. She can discourse on things tacky while wearing an evening gown with her jogging sneakers on; or, again, be overjoyed at the prospect of a trip to Paris: "And we'll never have to ask for french fried potatoes. They'll just come like that." While her husband, "Well, he's rich for a living." Or as he expresses it: "It's very difficult to do something if you don't need any money." All ends forgivingly for both couples, as the aggrieved wife concedes that they both "need something to regret," and the other husband concedes "I knew when I married that everyone would want to dance with you." "Civilized, charming, stylish . . . Very warm and most amusing . . . delicately interweaves laughter and romance."—N.Y. Times. "An amiable comedy about the eternal quadrangle . . . The author's most entertaining play in years."—N.Y. Daily News. "A beautiful weave of plot, character and laughs . . . It's delicious."—NBC-TV. (#674)

## LEND ME A TENOR
(Farce)
by KENNETH LUDWIG

4 male, 4 female

This is the biggest night in history of the Cleveland Grand Opera Company, for this night in September, 1934, world-famous tenor Tito Morelli (also known as "Il Stupendo") is to perform his greatest role ("Otello") at the gala season-opening benefit performance which Mr. Saunders, the General Manager, hopes will put Cleveland on the operatic map. Morelli is late in arriving--and when he finally sweeps in, it is too late to rehearse with the company. Through a wonderfully hilarious series of mishaps, Il Stupendo is given a double dose of tranquilizers which, mixed with all the booze he has consumed, causes him to pass out. His pulse is so low that Saunders and his assistant, Max, believe to their horror that he has died. What to do? What to do? Max is an aspiring singer, and Saunders persuades him to black up, get into Morelli's Otello costume, and try to fool the audience into thinking that's Il Stupendo up there. Max succeeds admirably, but the comic sparks really fly when Morelli comes to and gets into his other costume. Now we have *two* Otellos running around, in costume, and two women running around, in lingerie -- each thinking she is with Il Stupendo! A sensation on Broadway and in London's West End. "A jolly play."--NY Times. "Non-stop laughter"--Variety. "Uproarious! Hysterical!"--USA Today. "A rib-tickling comedy."--NY Post. (#667) **Posters.**

## POSTMORTEM
(Thriller)
by KENNETH LUDWIG

4 male, 4 female . Int..

Famous actor-manager and playwright William Gillette, best known for over a generation as Sherlock Holmes in his hugely-successful adaptation of Conan Doyle (which is *still* a popular play in the Samuel French Catalogue), has invited the cast of his latest revival of the play up for a weekend to his home in Connecticut, a magnificent pseudo-medieval, Rhenish castle on a bluff overlooking the Connecticut River. Someone is trying to murder William Gillette, and he has reason to suspect that it is one of his guests for the weekend. Perhaps the murderer is the same villain who did away with Gillette's fiancee a year ago if you believe, as does Gillette, that her death was not--as the authorities concluded--a suicide. Gillette's guests include his current ingenue/leading lady and her boyfriend, his Moriarty and his wife, and Gillette's delightfully acerbic sister. For the evening's entertainment Gillette has arranged a seance, conducted by the mysterious Louise Perradine, an actress twenty years before but now a psychic medium. The intrepid and more than slightly eccentric William Gillette has taken on, in "real life", his greatest role: he plans to solve the case *a la* Sherlock Holmes! The seance is wonderfully eerie, revealing one guest's closely-guarded secret and sending another into hysterics, another into a swoon, as Gillette puts all the pieces of the mystery together before the string of attempts on his life leads to a rousingly melodramatic finale. " shots in the dark and darkly held secrets, deathbed letters, guns and knives and bottles bashed over the head, ghosts and hiders behind curtains and misbegotten suspicions. There are moments when you'll jump. Guaranteed."--The Telegraph. (#18677)

# Other Publications for Your Interest

## *SOCIAL SECURITY*
### (LITTLE THEATRE—COMEDY)
### By ANDREW BERGMAN

#### 3 men, 3 women—Interior

This is a real, honest-to-goodness hit Broadway comedy, as in the Good Old Days of Broadway. Written by one of Hollywood's top comedy screenwriters ("Blazing Saddles" and "The Inlaws") and directed by the great Mike Nichols, this hilarious comedy starred Marlo Thomas and Ron Silver as a married couple who are art dealers. Their domestic tranquility is shattered upon the arrival of the wife's goody-goody nerd of a sister, her uptight CPA husband and her Archetypal Jewish Mother. They are there to try to save their college student daughter from the horrors of living only for sex. The comic sparks really begin to fly when the mother hits it off with the elderly minimalist artist who is the art dealers' best client! "Just when you were beginning to think you were never going to laugh again on Broadway, along comes *Social Security* and you realize, with a rising feeling of joy, that it is once more safe to giggle in the streets. Indeed, you can laugh out loud, joyfully, with, as it were, social security, for the play is a hoot, and better yet, a sophisticated, even civilized hoot."—NY Post.                                                   (#21255)

## *ALONE TOGETHER*
### (LITTLE THEATRE—COMEDY)
### By LAWRENCE ROMAN

#### 4 men, 2 women—Interior

Remember those wonderful Broadway comedies of the fifties and sixties, such as *Never Too Late* and *Take Her, She's Mine*? This new comedy by the author of *Under the Yum Yum Tree* is firmly in that tradition. Although not a hit with Broadway's jaded critics, *Alone Together* was a delight with audiences. On Broadway Janis Paige and Kevin McCarthy played a middle aged couple whose children have finally left the nest. They are now alone together—but not for long. All three sons come charging back home after experiencing some Hard Knocks in the Real World—and Mom and Dad have quite a time pushing them out of the house so they can once again be *alone together*. "Mr. Roman is a fast man with a funny line."—Chr. Sci. Mon. "A charmer."—Calgary Sunday Sun. "An amiable comedy . . . the audience roared with recognition, pleasure and amusement."—Gannett Westchester Newsp. "Delightfully wise and witty." Hollywood Reporter. "One of the funniest shows we've seen in ages."—Herald-News. TV.                                                   (#238)

# Other Publications for Your Interest

## *KNOCK KNOCK*

### (LITTLE THEATRE—FARCE)

### By JULES FEIFFER

#### 3 men, 1 woman—Composite interior

Take a pair of old Jewish bachelor recluses, throw in Joan of Arc who also in another life was Cinderella—add another character who appears in various guises and you have the entire cast but not the story of this wild farce. Cohn, an atheistic ex-musician is the housekeeper "half" of this "odd couple." Abe, an agnostic ex-stockbroker is the practical "half." They have lived together for twenty years—are bored to tears with one another and constantly squabble. Cohn, exasperated, wishes for intelligent company and on the scene enters one Wiseman who appears in many roles and is part Mephistopheles, part Groucho Marx. Then Joan of Arc appears before the couple telling them her mission is to recruit two of every species for a spaceship trip to heaven. After that all antic hell breaks loose and continues to the mad ending. ". . . a wild spree of jokes . . . helium-light laughter."—Clive Barnes, N.Y. Times. ". . . a kooky, laugh-saturated miracle play in the absurdist tradition."—Time. ". . . grand fun, possessed by a bright madness . . ."—N.Y. Post. ". . . a knockout of original humor."—NBC. ". . . intelligent and very funny play."—WABC-TV.

## *LITTLE MURDERS*

### (ALL GROUPS—COMEDY)

### By JULES FEIFFER

#### 6 men, 2 women—Interior

"Jules Feiffer, a satirical sharpshooter with a deadly aim, stares balefully at the meaningless violence in American life, and opens fire on it in 'Little Murders.' . . . Can be devastatingly lethal in some of its coldly savage comic assaults." (N.Y. Post). The play is really a collection of what Walter Kerr called set pieces, showing us a modern metropolitan family of matriarchal mother, milquetoast father, normal cuddly sister, and brother who is trying to adapt himself to homosexuality. Sister's fiance is a fellow who knows how to roll with the punches; he figures that if you daydream while being mugged, it won't hurt so much. They have a hard time finding a preacher who will marry them without pronouncing the name of God. But they succeed, to their sorrow. For immediately afterward sister is killed by a sniper's bullet. A detective who has a stack of unsolved crimes suspects that there is "a subtle pattern" forming here. "'Little Murders' is fantastically funny. You will laugh a lot."—N.Y. Times. "You have made me laugh, you have made me collapse. I want to go back."—N.Y. Post. "One of the finest comedies this season.—NBC-TV.